The Base Jumpers and Other Stories

Copyright Leif Gregersen July 2, 2014

Other works by Leif Gregersen:

"Through The Withering Storm: A Brief History of a Mental Illness"

"Green Mountain Road and Selected Stories"

"Poems From Inside Me

First White of Winter Poems

All four books available at amazon.com or by contacting
The author, lgregersen@ymail.com
Join me on Facebook at Valhalla Books
For regular free samples of my writing

| The Base Jumpers and Other Stories

Leif Gregersen

This book is dedicated to Raevn, Donna, Mira, Caroline, and my departed mother Beverly, each of whom contributed greatly to my writing ambitions more than any could know, and to my Father Leif Gregersen Senior for being the most incredible Dad ever, well into his golden years.

The Base Jumpers and Other Stories

Leif Gregersen

THE BASE JUMPERS

The two young men sat on the ground with their backs up against a pine tree. The view of the surrounding mountains was incredible thought the first of the two, Josh as he adjusted his scarf and zipped up his jacket to the very top to keep out the chill. The second member of the two-man team was taking long pulls from a hand-rolled cigarette of questionable origin and he wasn't sure what he felt about his surroundings. If you asked Brad, who had long hair and likely hadn't shaved in a week what he felt about the view that surrounded him he might say it was 'trippy'.

"So you're telling me then," Josh said to Brad, "that I might as well forget it, that she's about to play the 'I only want to be friends card' on me."

"That's exactly what I'm saying dude." Brad replied. "Maria just isn't your kind of girl. She's the kind of girl that likes men who are dangerous, who are experienced, confident. Like…"

"Like you." Josh said, sounding a bit dejected.

"You said it mano, I didn't. Hey listen-" Brad paused for another pull on the smelly, smoking thing in his hand, then continued. "I've known you for ten years dude and…"

"And you still haven't discovered I have a name other than dude."

"Sorry dude… I… oh crap!" Brad started laughing like the most hilarious thing he had ever seen had just taken place as he coughed out thick smoke, which made Josh want to strangle him. Still, they were there to have fun, and in all reality, Brad was a good friend. At the very least he had been his best friend for longer than anyone else had stayed by his side.

"Okay man, finish that thing and let's go…"

"I'm done." Brad replied and flicked away his pleasure making device. The two ran out and jumped right off the edge of a cliff that was twenty feet away from where they had been sitting. For the first couple of seconds nothing could be heard but Josh's screaming as they fell the 8,000 feet into the canyon below. What seemed like ten lifetimes passed and then at around 3,000 feet their parachutes opened and then whipped them upwards as they filled with air and then gently brought them down into a bunch of trees.

Brad landed on the edge of a rock and instantly sprained both his ankles. He was the lucky one, Josh went into a pine tree and pulled his groin all out of kilter rather seriously. Luckily this time they had thought to have someone meet them in the canyon with a truck, otherwise they would have made an unsightly pair hobbling or even crawling off towards whatever kind of medical assistance they felt they needed. They had radios but those were last resorts and there was no guarantee the rescue helicopter could get to them in bad weather which could happen at any time. Not to mention that they weren't really supposed to be base jumping in this national park.

Their ride came and had a good laugh at the two. This kind of thing was happening all the time, and it kept his larder stocked with all the money crazy kids would pay to play these games. He was just happy no one was killed- this time.

Over the next few days the two had a lot of chances to talk as they shared a semi-private room in the local hospital in Jasper. It was a good thing too, because the staff had a generally poor attitude towards perfectly healthy young kids who had to go off and kill themselves on motorbikes and hang gliders and parachutes all for what they considered stupid thrills.

"Let me tell you man," Brad said to Josh who could barely move from the pain that even morphine didn't totally knock out. "I'm through with all this. You, me- we're smart, we're young. We need to get out and make some money. Get this-before I came on this trip I was talking to my Uncle. He said that there is a lot of opportunity in pawn shops these days. Instead of us buying and selling everything one season to buy all the diving and skiing and whatever gear we need for the next season, we can set up a kind of pawn shop that specializes in extreme sports equipment. We can deal in a few ounces of silver and the odd gold ring, maybe a camera or two. But we mainly buy and sell sports equipment, and we make money each time something comes in or goes out of the store."

"What about your little problem? Seems to me you can't seem to help getting high all the time, that doesn't make for good business." Josh stated.

"If it means that much to you dude, I'll quit. I'll even go to rehab for three weeks out at Henwood when we get back to town. If that doesn't sound like I'm serious about this I don't know what does." Came Brad's reply.

"You mean it? But you're the worst chronic I've ever seen. Do you seriously think you can do it?" Josh asked him.

"I know I can. I don't need that garbage. What I need is money. Money to eat out, money to go skiing, money to take trips and buy a decent car. I'm sick of all this scrounging so we can go make a base jump and end up like this, broke all over again because we couldn't afford to go jump in some decent place. We'll be lucky if we can pay our rent this month!" Brad said.

For the first time in the years Josh had known him, Brad seemed to be talking sense. It was a no-brainer that he wasn't happy about the pain he was in. "So where do we come up with the money to start this all up? We need rent, inventory, charge and debit accounts, heat, power, water. Probably even a bookkeeper."

"I've got it all figured out dude."

"Stop calling me dude or I'm going to end this idea now." Josh said through a haze of pain.

"Josh my friend, my Uncle believes in me. He's going to co-sign a loan for the two of us. All we have to do is clear $2200 a month and we'll have all the bills paid and we'll be out of debt in just a couple of years. And we'll be working towards something, going somewhere. Remember how many times you complained you think your Dad loses all respect for you whenever you go to him for another handout? Well that will stop, along with a lot of other problems, including how your girlfriend feels for you."

"I don't know if I should make a decision like this on this much pain killer." Josh said. "But it does sound pretty damn good."

"Take all the time you need bro."

"Don't call me bro either. I'm your business partner, not your friend anymore."

A few weeks went by, Brad got out of the hospital but his Uncle Marvin came for a visit a few times and talked things over. One day Brad went with him to his car and when he came back to the room he looked dejected.

"Josh man, I think we might have a bit of a problem." Brad said.

"What's going on? Did your Uncle change his mind?"

"No, not really. Well, things are like this. He said that with all the crazy stuff we do and the things we get into he wants to have some guarantee. He said he wants us to take out insurance on each other with each other as the beneficiary and him as the next in line for it just in case. He made it sound like it was a deal-killer."

"Well that doesn't sound that bad. How much will it cost?"

"Not much, maybe another $200 a month on top of the $2200 we talked about. That would cover us each for about a million." Brad said looking despondent.

"That's nothing man, we can do that. I heard of all kinds of business people who have to take out insurance." Josh said and saw Brad's face go back to somewhat normal.

"Thanks man, you won't ever regret trusting me."

"I regret it already!" Josh said, smiling, but something in Brad's eyes made him feel that maybe he wasn't all that far off his mark.

The next few days went by fairly quickly. Soon it was time for Brad to go back to Edmonton and check himself into the treatment centre for 3 weeks. Hopefully by that time Josh would be through with his physiotherapy and be ready to start looking for a spot for their shop. They needed something near the University on Whyte Avenue to bring in buyers, but they also needed to find a way to compromise their choice of location because they would also need a steady stream of sellers of used equipment. No matter how many calls they made or how many times they crunched the numbers, they just couldn't find a way to get a store on Whyte. That meant they were going to have to figure a way to bring traffic to themselves. Josh told Brad just to worry about getting on his feet first though and the two friends parted with a fist bump.

Brad got back to the apartment the two had shared before leaving for their fateful base jump and instead of calling the Alcohol and Drug Abuse Commission like he was supposed to, he called up Maria, the girl Josh liked and invited her over under the pretense Josh would be there later. She arrived and he answered the door with a bottle of wine and two glasses in his hand.

"Hey Brad. How's your foot doing?" Maria said and walked in the apartment past him.

"Both feet. They hurt a little, they're weak, but they work now at least. How you been?" Brad said in a kind of sultry voice.

Maria plopped herself on the couch and picked up a magazine. She tossed it away with an "ewww" when she discovered it wasn't the kind of magazine that should have been left sitting out. "When is Josh getting here? I kind of miss that guy."

"Josh is where he always is, off in his own little world. He might not even make it back tonight, he said he was going to cruise the bars a bit." Brad lied. "Want a drink?"

"Yeah, I guess I could have a glass. What do you mean cruise the bars?" Maria asked sounding a bit angry.

"Well, that's what he said. He goes out every now and then, doesn't get lucky every time but doesn't do too bad. Better than me." Brad poured some wine in Maria's glass and set down the bottle and started to rub her shoulders. Maria moaned.

"Oh, I've been needing a decent neck rub all week. Is that all Josh said?"

"Yeah, pretty much. Sometimes I don't see him for days."

"You know him and I were becoming a thing don't you?" Maria asked him.

"No, I didn't know. Does that effect our relationship?" Brad asked sounding innocent.

"I don't know. Pour me some more wine and start working my back and we'll talk." Brad smiled a greasy smile and hoped the wine was going to do its job.

Time passed and Josh's freedom of movement slowly got better. That was one great thing about the hospital in Jasper, they were used to treating things like groin injuries. He had tried to call Maria a couple of times but she didn't answer and didn't call him back. He wondered how Brad was doing in Henwood treatment centre but didn't worry too much. Josh didn't trust Brad completely, but he knew that if there was a chance of him finding a way to snowboard and travel all winter by working a few easy months in the summer, he would find it. The business would be a success, it was a good time to open a place like this. Josh even thought that he could make up a good side business renting different kinds of equipment, a lot of people rented their skis in town and then went off to different resorts. The trick was to charge a lot, but less than what a resort would charge for a lower quality rental. He just didn't know how they were going to get the word out about the shop.

After about three weeks had passed, Brad phoned up Josh in the hospital and it looked like in another couple of days Josh would be good to go home. Brad didn't say much about the treatment centre. He even sounded a bit high but Josh figured now that he had gone through what he had to it was more likely he could handle a puff now and then. Maybe he was still 'permafried' from his years of use. He asked about Maria and Brad told him that he was now seeing her officially. He had expected that, Brad had always gotten the nice looking and decent ones. Trouble was six months later they were chain smoking alcoholics with an attitude and then Brad would just move on to the next victim. Josh had really thought Maria was better than that.

Josh rode the train home and Brad picked him up at the Via Rail station. Most of his pain was gone and he was practically paranoid about taking things like morphine or even codeine so he just dealt with his pain. The first thing he talked to Brad about was how to get the word out. Brad told him that his Uncle suggested they perform some kind of publicity stunt or run a TV commercial to get the word out and Brad told him the idea he came up with.

"It's simple Josh." That was maybe the third time in his life he had been called by name from Brad. "We're going to get a banner sign and parachute into Edmonton with it. We'll hire someone with a camera to film us going down and that will be our TV commercial. What do you think?"

"It rocks. Give me a couple of weeks to get to the gym and the pool and I can do it. Just promise me the pilot knows enough to stay away from forests when he drops us off."

"Deal dude." Brad said.

"Josh. Dude."

Over the next few days Brad would go out every now and then for a few hours and not say where he would be. One day Josh got sick of wondering what was going on and followed him out and discovered not only had he not stopped with the smoke, he was seeing Maria and probably trying to keep her from talking to him. Just four days before they were going to shoot their commercial, Josh waited until Brad left her place and then buzzed in and started talking with Maria.

That night Josh went home but said very little to Brad. He asked a few details about what had been put in place for the business, when the loan would be transferred to their business account and so on. Finally, Josh went out to the storage garage they had rented when they moved into their apartment and got their parachutes. He made sure to let Brad know he would be gone all day the next day and asked him to check over everything. The two parachutes were easy to tell apart, though they were the same make and model, they had attached a yellow name patch to Brad's and a red one to Josh's.

Soon came the day to head off to the airfield North of Edmonton in Villeneuve. They met the cameraman there and for some reason Brad said he had forgotten to pack a third headset radio for the cameraman. Still, it wasn't any kind of safety issue, so they got the okay from the pilot and the parachute club to go ahead. The sky was clear and the weather was warm.

Josh noticed that Brad seemed kind of nervous, that he kept fidgeting, checking his parachute straps, moving around. He asked him if he had forgotten to use the bathroom, but he said he was fine. The pilot climbed up to 10,000 feet-the highest you can go without bringing oxygen and gave a wave of his hand to signal all was good. Josh and Brad climbed out on the wing spar and turned on their headset radios and the cameraman clung to the door, ready to jump when they did. When all seemed right, the three of them all went at once.

"Brad, I have something to say to you." Josh said slowly and coldly over the radios they wore as they unfolded the sign and were all smiles for the camera.

"What's that Josh?"

"I know what you said and did with Maria. I know what you did to my parachute."

"What? What do you know? I didn't do anything."

"I know you tampered with it, and subtly enough that it will look like an accident. I just have one thing to say after I pull my rip cord."

"What's that?"

"Maria really loves ME and she is a great seamstress. She switched the patches on our chutes and you couldn't even tell. Goodbye DUDE."

Josh pulled his chute, and then so did the cameraman, but Brad's chute just seemed to fizzle in mid-air, didn't open at all. Josh watched him fall.

There was a brief investigation but nothing conclusive was found. Josh went ahead and started up the business, he had no problem borrowing the money directly from the bank instead of Brad's Uncle because he had evidence of insurance money coming in. The business turned out to a great idea and it did really well. In a short time he received a cheque from the insurance company for a million dollars and paid off his loans and thought nothing of spending $30,000.00 on a wedding with Maria. He pretty much had to marry her, after all she was his accomplice and could have turned him in. She never did though, and they went on to have three wonderful, non-extreme sporting kids. Their kids were popular growing up because their Dad could always get their friends a deal on any kind of sporting gear they needed. Josh never felt any remorse about what he had done and so he lived out his days in happiness with the woman he most cared for in the world.

THE END

Leif Gregersen

Henry Jensen

*****Edmonton, Alberta, Canada, late winter, 2014*****

Henry Jensen sat on his couch watching TV in his small and sparse bachelor apartment. He rented his place through a local church in the city of Edmonton, not far from 118 avenue. The locals called 118 avenue: "The avenue of nations" because of the diversity of cultures and religions there. Most of the people that lived along the avenue knew it as "The avenue of abominations", and it was easy to see why. There were gangs, there was prostitution, loud motorcycles and no one in their right mind would walk down the street at night.

The building Henry Jensen lived in was called Avenue United Manor and had an air of comfort and cleanliness to it that can only be achieved with tenants who put time and effort into making the place where they lived clean, quiet and well kept up. It didn't hurt that at both main entrances there was a Billy club handy near the door in case it might be needed. It also helped that the building had thoughtful owners, in this case a local United Church whose staff weighed carefully the interests and comfort of the building's tenants in all decisions.

Henry did have issues with the building management, everything from them coming in unannounced into his apartment, to changing the rules all the time to suit themselves. Still, for a single elderly person on a pension it was a pretty nice place to live, and it was fairly inexpensive. Apartments in Edmonton like his could easily go for twice the $400.00 a month he paid here, and he was just barely scraping by as it was. He had been out of work some time before retiring and hadn't been able to save anything, and so he felt that living here was a lot better than some of the alternatives, like living off his son or daughter.

Today was a Tuesday, around the middle of the month, the time when most pensioners were broke and waiting for their next cheque. Henry, or Hank as he was better known, called up an old friend ten minutes after he woke up and dressed and had his breakfast.

"Hello Carl!" Hank said.

"Hank! I didn't know you were smart enough to use a telephone." His friend Carl said.

"I could operate a damn tank if I wanted and you know it."

"Hard to operate a vehicle without a license." Carl said.

"Listen Carl, are you going to wisecrack or are you going to come over and watch the hockey game with me tonight?"

"No need to get touchy! I'll be there at six and maybe I'll bring some pizza from my son's restaurant."

"Okay, but bring us ham and pineapple this time and none of that spicy sauce you like so much." Hank said.

"Sure thing my good friend. See you tonight then. And wipe off the TV screen, that thing must be coated in twenty years of cigarette smoke!"

It was going to be nice to have a little company, Hank thought, especially someone who had known him since his younger days.

Canadian Corps Headquarters, England, spring 1944

"Sergeant Jensen!" The tall and immaculately groomed officer said. "I need to see you in my office."

"Yes Sir." The Sergeant said. Hank Jensen followed Lieutenant East to his office, then went in with him and closed the door.

"Sit down Hank, I need you to take a look at these maps and for now try to commit them to memory."

"Yes Sir, may I ask what these are for?"

"As you know Sergeant, the invasion of France is coming sooner rather than later. Right now everything is cloaked in secrecy, if we let out even the slightest peep of the date or location to the enemy, it will be an utter disaster. You see those two hills on the upper part of the map?"

"Yes Sir." Hank said, trying to focus on all the details of the landscape the map represented.

"We're going to put you and about 27 other men down in an Airspeed Horsa glider just south of those two hills. We know it's not your normal job, and that they aren't even your men, but you will be in command of them, and perhaps more importantly, you will be in charge of the safety of a high-ranking officer. From your landing zone you will head west, about three miles, where the officer will take charge of a group of men who are to lay down some safe zones for our infantry and tanks coming inland."

"May I ask Sir, which officer will I be guarding on this babysitting mission?" Hank said.

"Same person who took you from being a Lieutenant like me to the Sergeant you are, Colonel Pearson."

"God help me." Sergeant Jensen said.

*****Edmonton, Alberta, Canada Late winter, 2014*****

Hank flipped from channel to channel until finally he was nearly blasted out of his seat by the buzzer at the door. That damn thing is worse than an air raid siren he thought to himself. With a bit of effort, he got up and walked to the intercom.

"We don't want any and I gave at the office." Hank said.

"Are you sure? How do you know I'm not Mae West?" Came the reply.

"Because of your wrinkled old lemon face." Hank said, and pushed the buzzer to let him in.

Hank's friend Carl came in and the pair sat down to eat and joke around with each other. They enjoyed their evening, and Hank enjoyed his meal, except for the fact that the pizza sauce, though he promised it was the mild kind, hit Hank's stomach hard like an unexpected punch.

The game was exciting, Edmonton made a good showing, the Kings barely even beat them, which cost Hank $20 for the bet they always made. When he handed it over, Hank felt that awful feeling he would often get when he was once again running out of money before he ran out of month. Next time he would have to bet against Edmonton he thought, and though his worries seemed to add to the sore feeling in his stomach, he tried not to think too much about it and went to bed soon after Carl left.

In the middle of the night, Hank woke up and the pain in his stomach was worse. He chalked it up to the pizza sauce and got up to use the bathroom and possibly get some antacid if he had any. On his way there his stomach did a double take and he got sick all over the floor-but the worst part of it was that he was throwing up blood. It scared him to think that he had gone through a war and raising a family and all those years of working in car sales to end up like this. He put aside his tough guy instinct and called the hospital. They were eager to send an ambulance right away.

"Mr. Jensen, have you been in hospital before for your stomach?" One of the paramedics asked, and he seemed somehow to drift away and passed out on the gurney as they took him into the ambulance, limp and blood coming from his mouth.

*****Bristol Filton Airport, England, June 5, 1944*****

A massive tent had been erected for the men who would be going over early the next morning for operation Overlord, also known as D-Day. There was a gentle rain hitting the ceiling of the tent that made many of the men think of better days, times when they didn't have to face something so frightening and difficult for such an important cause. They had yet to even board their aircraft but all of them looked like they had been through the wars. Anxiety, lack of sleep, and not knowing even if they would survive the next few days or what they would really be like had taken it's toll on the men. When all of the glider troops in the regiment were assembled Colonel Pearson got up on a podium to speak to them.

"Gentlemen, our task is not a simple one. Unlike our brothers in the Airborne, the glider forces going over don't feel it is logical to jump out of a perfectly good airplane. We are going to ride our vehicles to the ground. Our gliders have the advantage of silence and surprise, and the double power of having our tow planes inflict further casualties upon the enemy. I don't want to lie to you, the odds are not in the favor of any particular man making it through. I have gone over our objectives with all the squad leaders and platoon leaders, and I have let them know we have a tough fight ahead of us. After that, God willing, we will be on foreign soil and will be facing a bloodied and toughened enemy who will dog us at every turn. But what I have to say to you this day is that the people of Europe, and the people of the world are watching because ours is an incredibly necessary job, despite all of the risk. As the commander of Airborne Infantry Group A113 I will be with you right on the ground. We will face down the enemy, and we will be victorious!" As he said this last word, a cheer rose up for England, another for Canada, and a third for Colonel Pearson. Then, in groups of their individual glider teams, the men were led off to board their aircraft and wait.

"Alright you men, follow me. Stay together, I don't want to have to look for you." Sergeant Jensen said to his glider contingent. "Colonel Pearson Sir, if you would join us."

"You?" The Colonel said. "Don't tell me you are on my glider. I thought I had dealt with you enough already."

"Sir, all I know is you requested the best man available to get you to your rendez-vous point and I'm it. I fought in North Africa, Sicily, Italy and trained hard to get these Sergeant's stripes. I also have spent the past weeks making the men who will be protecting you into a solid, cohesive force of trained killers. We will take good care of you Sir, that's a promise."

"Very well then Sergeant, but I will be watching you. Any sign of disrespect or negligence and I can assure you there will be a court martial." Colonel Pearson said.

The Base Jumpers and Other Stories

Sergeant Jensen winced. If only you had given me a chance back in England, this wouldn't be such a difficult job he thought.

The 28 men boarded their glider and Sergeant Jensen briefed them on their mission. Some of the men were sick with nerves but joked and bantered all the same. Then when their tow-planes started their engines and they began to move all went silent. Each soldier checked and rechecked each piece of equipment they would need from the action on their Enfield rifles to the moving parts on their entrenching tools and light machine guns. There was no more faking it now, ten minutes ago they were boys playing at soldiers, now they were men who had to be completely professional warriors.

Edmonton, Alberta, Canada, late winter, 2014

"H.. . h... ow long will I have to stay here Doctor?" Hank said when his surgeon came to see him two weeks after he had arrived.

"We don't really know for sure Mr. Jensen." The Doctor said.

Leif Gregersen

"Hank- please call me Hank."

"I'm sorry Hank, you lost a lot of blood and we had to operate on your ulcer. For the past while you have been a bit disoriented, so I don't know if talking about releasing you is the best thing right away, we have to see how you do. I think in another week if your levels get back up we can consider sending you home, but we will have to see. And I think you have to seriously look at getting into a place to live with more care then where you are at."

Hank wished he had words to say how much he hated that idea, how to him that was just like digging his own grave. He thought of friends that had gone to such places and just sat staring at the walls and occasionally getting their diapers changed. He missed his wife, now 5 years gone. He missed his kids, now far away. But he wouldn't ask them for help if he could. Before he could think much more about everything he drifted off to sleep and dreamed of a sunny summer day with his dear departed love, having a picnic in their favorite park by the river.

A week passed and Hank ended up being released. He was given a list of foods to eat and another to not eat and he got the receptionist at the hospital to call him a cab. He got to his building and let himself into the front door and then went to open the door to his apartment and his key no longer worked. He stormed off to the manager's office and banged hard on his door.

"What the hell is going on? My key won't fit my door!" Hank said.

"Your key won't fit your door because you didn't pay your rent and I evicted you." The caretaker said.

"Evicted? What in the world for?"

"You didn't pay your rent is what for."

"My rent gets paid directly, it goes right from my pension cheque to your administration! "

"We didn't get it this month. You were gone and someone said you were carried off not moving into an ambulance, bleeding, so we figured you died."

"Well I'm not dead, I'm here right here now. Let me into my place and I'll write you a cheque for the rent!"

"Sorry can't do it. Company policy." Hank started to turn green and grabbed the caretaker by his collars.

"Listen you little bastard. I'm not afraid of you. I killed a hundred of your type over in Europe and I'm not past killing one more. Now let me into my apartment!" Hank said, with an almost crazy look to his face. The caretaker gulped and swallowed and the second Hank let him go he disappeared into his office. He locked himself in and Hank banged on the door. In a few short minutes the police came and the caretaker buzzed them in and only came out when they could protect him from this frail but angry old man.

"Are you the guy who called us about the assault?" One of the cops asked the caretaker.

"Yes, I would like to charge this person. I legally evicted him and he just threatened to kill me and grabbed me by the collars."

"That's right and I would do it again, he evicted me by mistake when I was in the hospital and won't let me get my chequebook and pay the rent."

"I'm sorry Sir, but if he evicted you he can do that. He can even sell your stuff to pay the rent you owe. I suggest you get a Lawyer, and I suggest to you," The cop said and pointed at the caretaker, "stop being such an asshole."

"So what do I do now then?" Hank asked him.

"We can give you a ride to the shelter where you can stay for free until you find another place."

"Well, I guess you're the law in this case. Thank you for being kind." Hank said. "And you- I'll be back." He said to the caretaker.

*****Over Normandy, France, June 6th, 1944*****

"Alright men, we are now over the beaches of the English channel. Below us is massing an invasion force the size of which mankind has never seen." Sergeant Jensen said. "Now that we are underway I can tell you that the landings will be in Normandy and our job has been set out to protect Colonel Pearson and to deliver him to the commanders of the main glider force at all costs, safe and sound. As you may know, a Colonel is a valuable target to the enemy and I want to say to you that if all of us get hit so the Colonel can make it, it means we have done the job we were set aside for."

The men looked somber in their hard and uncomfortable canvas seats. Some crossed themselves, some tried to joke their way through. Occasionally one would get sick in buckets that had been provided.

Soon the pilot of the huge glider hit a switch that turned on an indicator light telling the men to get ready for landing. The tow-rope was released with a thump and the glider floated free, the only sound being the rushing wind that told them they were moving, added with a sensation of descending. The men braced themselves as the ground got closer and then all of a sudden they knew they were in deep trouble.

Somehow it seemed, the glider had overshot its' landing point. The super light structure made mostly of wood banged into and bashed around in what seemed to be a forest. With a loud crash and a bone-splitting "thump" a fifteen foot section of one wing broke off as they slid through the trees. Then the glider must have hit something solid, an old stone house or a creek bank or something, because it violently flipped over leaving a tangle of arms and legs before the ordeal was finally over and the glider stopped moving.

"Alright men, if you are injured, don't cry out. We don't know how many Germans are around us or where we landed yet. Check your buddies beside you if you can, help them out if they are hurt!" Hank said.

"Sergeant Jensen!" The Colonel said.

"Yes Sir, what do you need?" Sergeant Jensen said.

"Sergeant, my foot is caught in something and I can't move it."

"Can you hold tight Sir, I want to count up the dead and wounded and assess what needs to be done."

"By all means Sergeant." The Colonel said.

Hank took out his flashlight and first went up front. There he witnessed the most gruesome sight he had ever seen. What seemed like a tree branch on a tree that had probably stood for 600 years had been pushed through the front window of the glider and had broken the pilot's neck. After trying to shake the shock of this image out of his head, he went back to where his men and the Colonel were in the overturned glider, and it seemed no one had gotten off as easy as he did. He tallied up the damage and learned that seven men were dead, most with broken necks or head trauma and the rest had broken bones, some of them multiple broken bones and even broken backs so he spent the next hour dragging out the dead, and trying to set and brace what injuries he could for the living as silently as possible. An hour was all he dared take, working as quickly and carefully as he could, because he knew that soon Germans would be trying to round up all Allied forces near the landing and drop zones. Hank took stock of the usable weapons and equipment they had and set up a defensive perimeter of machine gun placements. There was no time to entrench them, he just put men that could still use their arms in a few spots and set up the guns for them as he could. When the enemy came, they would at least in some small way be ready for them. Trying to move them didn't seem to be an option.

Edmonton, Alberta, Canada, late winter, 2014

"So what you are telling me is the cheque has been cashed." Hank said to the Veteran's Affairs officer in Ottawa over the phone at the shelter.

"We have an indication here that your rent payment was sent and that your remaining pension cheque was also sent and that both cheques were cashed." The case worker said.

"But what I'm trying to tell you is that I was in the hospital and I can prove it. And I can also prove that the caretaker has cashed my cheque and now I have no place to stay!" Hank said.

"And what I'm trying to tell you is that you can file a complaint and after an investigation if what you say is true you will be issued another cheque."

"So what do I do now then? Do you understand I'm living in a filthy shelter? I have no money to even do my laundry or a towel to take a shower with. Do you realize this place is filled with diseases and cockroaches and bedbugs? What the hell do you expect me to do about that?" Hank heard a click. "Hello? Hello?" Then he slammed down the phone. Son of a bitch he thought to himself. After all I've done!

Hank took to wandering the streets during day to kill time. For a while he tried going to the library but he got a lot of evil glares and the occasional warning from the security guards there. He would get hungry but he didn't like to beg anything from anyone, so his weight kept dropping. A couple of days later the flu started to hit people at the shelter hard, with two people ending up in the hospital and just about everyone hacking up green phlegm on the sidewalk out front. He called up his friend Carl who lived in a lodge and couldn't have overnight guests. One thing he did help with was a thick blanket he didn't need and Hank decided it was safer to live under a bridge than in that diseased, disgusting shelter. The weather had been warming up anyway, and after all, he had slept outside all through France and Germany on foot.

Soon after Hank started sleeping outside though, he found he slept very poorly and that his old bones weren't used to such hardships like they once were. The last straw was when he started coughing up blood again.

Finally, just a week from getting his benefits again Hank simply gave up. He had something, one thing, that he had carried with him that he would never part with but could use to get a little comfort for himself. He walked into a pawn shop and took it out.

*****Forest outside Bayeax, France, June 6, 1944*****

"Sir, we are going to have to get you out of here." Hank said.

"Well that's bloody well obvious. But how, with my foot under that twisted metal?" The Colonel said.

"You're not going to like this but I'll be as gentle as I can. I think I see a way to do it." The Colonel's face went ashen.

"You mean you want to…"

"Yes Sir, I think you know we have to break your foot to get it out."

"Damn you Sergeant! Damn you and your logic! Well, let's get this done then!"

Hank took his Thompson submachine gun and slid it under the Colonel's trapped foot. Without any countdown or stalling, he simply pulled hard on the end of the gun and the Colonel's foot twisted in an unnatural angle and with some stifled moans of pain and a quick application of force to pull it out, the Colonel's foot slid from under the metal that had trapped it.

"Son of Beelzebub that hurts!" The Colonel said, grimacing.

"Now I want you to get on my back Sir." Hank said.

"On this side?"

"No Sir, that side is a bit tender. If you could try the left side."

"My God man, you mean to tell me…"

"Yes Sir, I dislocated my right shoulder in the crash. But it didn't matter because you and the others needed my help."

"I won't forget this Sergeant."

"Neither will I Sir."

The Germans attacked the glider landing point many times that day but the men held fast. Sadly though, after the third attack which was supported by German artillery, the remaining men were either killed or captured. The two men who survived were decorated for bravery and the merit of holding their position while the Colonel made his way to his command post. Perhaps what was more important though, was that, despite his injury, Sergeant Henry Jensen managed to carry Colonel Pearson to his destination, some 17 miles from where their glider crashed. Thanks to the fallen and the injured, Colonel Pearson was able to successfully lead the glider force to help the invasion force to establish a proper beachhead. The Colonel's thankfulness to Henry Jensen from then on knew no bounds. He was reinstated at his former rank, and after a short stay in a hospital in England, was able to return to duty which he carried out skillfully until the end of the war.

*****Edmonton, Alberta, Canada, late Winter, 2014*****

"Can I help you Sir?" The pawnshop owner asked.

"I would like to see if I can get a loan." Hank said.

"What do you have there?"

"It's a Victoria Cross."

"Victoria Cross? I'm sorry, we don't usually deal in medals, and we have found so many fakes of that one in particular. As you may know, it's the highest honor in the British Empire. Why, it's so high up they even stopped giving it to Canadians a few years ago."

"I can assure you this one is quite real." Hank said.

"Do you have any documentation for it?"

"Yes of course. Here." Hank said and unfolded then handed over a yellowed old piece of paper and also took from his wallet two small photographs. The paper said:

This document is to confirm the authenticity of the Victoria Cross, given to Captain Henry Jensen, Princess Patricia's Canadian Light Infantry in a ceremony at Buckingham Palace by King George VI upon the first anniversary of the Allied Invasion of Normandy June 6, 1945.

"And who is this here in the picture?"

"That is King George VI with me, in my younger days."

"And in this other one?"

"That is Brigadier General Pearson, who while injured, led his men to, capture two essential bridges in Normandy and paved a path for hundreds of thousands of men. He was also quite a hero in Korea I understand. The person beside him is also me, with my Victoria Cross displayed." Hank said.

"What connection did you have with him?"

"He was the person that insisted I be awarded the Victoria Cross and allowed me to do something very important after the war." The pawnshop owner could do nothing but stand there stunned by this amazing man who had been through so much. He almost couldn't believe after all this time anyone could even be left who had played such an important role in Canada's history.

"And what was that important thing?"

"He rescinded his former distaste for me and let me marry his daughter."

"You do realize that I can't begin to afford to buy this off you." The pawnshop owner said.

"I just want to pawn it," Hank said, coughing, "and I'll come back for it when I get my pension cheque."

"What do you want for it?"

"What do they go for?"

"I've seen them go for anywhere from 50,000 to 200,000 dollars."

"Give me $1,000.00 but it better damn well be here when I get back. Otherwise what I do to you will make what we did to the Germans look like a spanking."

"Absolutely Sir, nothing too good for our Veterans."

Hank took his money and travelled to the south side of Edmonton where he got a room in the Strathcona Hotel on Whyte Avenue. By coincidence, this hotel was the same place he had stayed in over 70 years ago when waiting to leave for the army back at the beginning of the war. He asked for it, and by luck he even got the same room he had his then fiancée share with him, though the old hotel wasn't as clean as it was back in the 1940's.

It was right at the top of the list of things he had been warned not to eat or drink, but he couldn't help getting himself a couple of shots of whiskey in the bar downstairs from his room as his mind wandered through years of memories of good times and bad. He got a bottle at a nearby liquor store and stayed up that night drinking, feeling desperately alone and realizing that all the old friends were gone, all the battles were now forgotten, and Canada had elected a government that didn't seem to have learned anything from what he had done.

As he coughed more and more, Hank wrote a letter on hotel stationary to each of his children and then one to his family lawyer. In the letter to his lawyer, he included the pawn ticket, which he had signed over to his lawyer and in the letter gave instructions that his Victoria Cross be sold and the proceeds divided between his kids evenly. He felt forlorn and forgotten, but he completed his task by walking down the street to a convenience store, buying stamps, envelopes, and even a money order to send to the pawn shop if by any chance his letter didn't get through on time and he needed to renew his loan. Retired Captain Henry Jensen never made it back to his hotel, he was overcome by coughing and fell on the two block walk back and in the darkness he slipped away to join all of his fallen comrades in arms. The letters found their way to their recipients, and Hank Jensen finally found his way home.

THE END

REDEMPTION

Bill, at age nineteen sat in one of the back pews of the Anglican Church where he was attending funeral services. He was a tall kid, tall and large-something that had gotten him a long way in hockey and football and more recently, in intimidating anyone who got in his way. It had been five years since he had seen the inside of a church, and as the pallbearers carried the body of his grandmother inside her coffin down the centre isle he was more in a daze than any emotional state he could name. But just before the eulogy, the church organist played "Amazing Grace" which had been both his grandmother's and his own favorite hymn, back in the days when the two of them loved doing anything together, but especially attending church and singing. He could recall some of the words that he once sang with passion, "Amazing grace, how sweet the sound... That saved a wretch like me... I once was lost but now am found... Was blind but now I see." The old song choked him up a bit and he felt his eyes moisten, something he didn't want to happen. He was too much of a tough guy now. He didn't need him Mom on his case about school or a job or any teachers telling him he had to study some crap. Now that his grandmother was being buried he figured this would be about the last he would have to do with his family.

Bill couldn't help but think that most of this service was bullshit. The pastor didn't seem to know anything about his mother's mom. He went on and on like they were best friends but he had never known his grandmother to attend this church. He sat through the service, munched down on some of the reception after, said hellos and goodbyes to his cousins and Uncles and, as soon as he got outside he phoned up a buddy to meet him at the small room he rented that he called home. On the way he picked up two 40 ounce bottles of cheap beer and then went home to change and get the hell away from all these formalities. And so, life went on like normal for the next few weeks.

Bill got his money the same way his Mom did, from welfare. At some point way back in school he got in one too many fights and failed one too many classes and some Doctor labelled him with a learning disability and when it came time to get his own cheque at age 18, he had no trouble doing so. The only real problem he had was making that monthly cheque last until the next one. Bill had a girl too, but it seemed she only liked him because he was huge and scary looking and no one ever messed with her or him when they were out. She said she liked his curly blonde hair and that he was cute but they hadn't gotten to the point of co-habitating. He had a suspicion she was sleeping with someone else, but as long as she clung to him a couple of times a week and gave him what he wanted later that night he didn't really care.

His friend Eli was a good guy, solid guy. He would never screw a guy over except maybe if he needed a drink or a hoot. He sure as hell wouldn't rat a guy out and every time one of them or both of them had money it was a good time to celebrate with some beer. The problem came one night when they were at Eli's apartment. They had bought a six-pack with their pooled money and it just wasn't enough to give them a decent buzz.

"Shit man. I got an idea!" Bill said as he poured a few ounces of his beer into a glass that needed washing and pushed it over to his buddy who tipped the glass back without hesitation.

"Spill it. What's the plan?"

"I know where my Mom keeps her spare key to the apartment, it's just under a balcony that you can get to from outside."

"How does that help us, dude?" Eli asked him, sounding interested.

"She always has money. Especially now I think she must have gotten something from my grandma. We go in, take a few bucks and then we can score some weed and at least another flat." Eli's eyes widened at the thought of 24 beer and some hoots.

"Let's do it! Just don't take too much, dude." The pair got on their sneakers and headed out the door, making a beeline for the building Bill's Mom lived in.

They got to the place in minutes, excited and happy, having had just enough beer to keep their nerves calm but not enough to make them screw-ups. Bill grabbed the key, and waited outside his Mom's window to make sure the light was off and there was no stirring in the house.

"Okay, man. Wait here. You be the lookout. If anything funny goes on, toss a rock at the window and I'll book it." Eli gave a nod and Bill was through the outside door, which should have been locked but had been broken open a long time ago and was never fixed. Through that, there was just one lock to open on his Mom's door.

He got inside and everything was dark so he took out his cigarette lighter and illuminated the kitchen space where his Mom usually left her purse. There it was. He opened it and nearly shit himself. There must have been two thousand bucks in there. He figured his Mom must have finally hit the big win on the VLT machines. He wasn't greedy. He just took a mere $500 out and as he was doing it there was a thunk on the wall. He didn't know what it was, but it woke his Mom up and she yelled,

"Samantha, is that you?" Samantha was his Aunt. She knew where the key was, too.

"Yeah, it's me. Go back to sleep. I'm gonna watch some TV." Bill said, making his voice higher and just like his Aunt's. It was a skill he always knew would come in handy. If all went well he would get out and Samantha would be blamed for the theft. Suddenly a rock went: Smack! On the balcony window, and it cracked. He could see it. He bolted for the door but when he opened it there was someone on the other side. It was a guy his Mom saw now and then. All Bill could think to do was to punch him and then knock him down and run past him with the $500 loosely stuffed in his pocket.

"Let's go, let's go!" He yelled as he got out the front door of the building. They sped off down the street and in just seconds, his Mom's boyfriend Chuck was running after them. They got down the block and then Bill yelled, "Split up!" and the pair both turned away from each other and ran in opposite directions. Their ruse worked. They got enough distance going and then they each hid and Matt was evaded. Minutes after that happened, though, there were cops all over the place. The pair of desperados luckily made it to Eli's before the dogs were called out. They didn't stay there long, though, and with the $500 they didn't really want to. They took a bus downtown, each got a mickey of booze and sat in a park sipping away at their bottles trying to figure out their next step.

They didn't really think things over too well and so they made another stop at the liquor store. Every time a police car went by or they heard a dog barking they felt they needed more. They decided the safest place to go would be to Bill's girlfriend's house. She was the only one who would let them in at this point they figured. The pair walked mile after mile, across the High Level Bridge to the apartment his girlfriend rented and they tried to buzz the front door button of her suite to get in. There was no answer, and Bill had no idea if there was a spare key. He left Eli to keep buzzing and walked around the side of the building to see if he could wake her.

"Patty! Patty!" He yelled, "Wake up, I need to get in!" Even those few words were slurred. Finally, a light came on and she stuck her head out the window.

"Get lost, Bill. I've got my boyfriend over!"

"What? I thought I was your boyfriend!"

"Get real, Bill. You come here drunk twice a week to get laid and you think you own me? Go fuck yourself!" She said and slammed the window shut. Bill wouldn't take that for an answer and started throwing pebbles at the window. For some reason he thought if she just knew he was in trouble she would let him in.

Instead, she sent her boyfriend out to talk to him. The dude came around the corner after a few minutes of pebble tossing and said: "Hey, man! She doesn't want to talk to you anymore, okay? Why don't you go back to the bar and find another chick?"

In a drunken rage Bill hit his new competition with a flurry of fists and when he was knocked down he started to kick him and kick him. Even Eli tried to stop him but then with the sounds of sirens coming closer he took off, stumbling into the darkness. When the cops came, they had to fight Bill to stop him from laying a boot fuck on the poor guy. When he stopped, Patty's boyfriend wasn't moving, and Bill soon passed out in the back of the cop car he was taken to.

The trial was a short one. The charges were manslaughter (Patty's boyfriend Steven died while Bill was in Remand), theft, break and enter and assault. There was no real way to deny it. Bill's mother didn't attend the trial at all, but Patty came once and couldn't even look in Bill's eyes. They seemed so red and evil, full of hate. In the end, Bill got ten years and when the verdict was read, his face showed no emotion. Eli was never charged, Bill stayed faithful to the one friend he had left. His trip to prison was a solemn one, as he walked in the gates and into the cell that was to be his home for the next six years minimum he could feel the leering and perverted eyes sizing him up. He had heard prison stories, true ones from a great uncle he had who spent five years in Kingston Penitentiary, the most violent of all Canadian prisons. The Edmonton Maximum Security Prison seemed better than that. The inmates were allowed a TV and a stereo in their cell, and there were different rehabilitation programs. Bill had no stereo to bring in but Eli managed to get him a boom box so at least he had tunes.

Prison hardened Bill. Up until he got there he had been just a juvenile delinquent. Now he was a hopeless case. He soon discovered he could refuse the list of courses that had been recommended for him and just lay around all day until it was time to eat or work out, the latter of which became his obsession. Weights helped reduce the stress of life behind bars, something he desperately needed to have relieved. He also learned how to make prison home brew, and as long as he could sneak some fruit and sugar to his cell he was able to get drunk pretty much any time he wanted.

He had been there a year when the news came down the pike: all of his drinking added to the worrying he had done seemingly added up and one day he found himself doubled up over the toilet in his cell puking blood. He went to see the doctor and after a number of tests he was told his liver and stomach were in seriously bad shape.

In fact, the Doctor felt that if he didn't change his habits he would be dead before he could finish out his sentence, even with good behavior. Bill laughed it off and kept on drinking, but the blood and some pain kept coming which added to his worries, which added to his problem.

Not long after his diagnosis, Bill was walking off some stomach pains when he took a route he didn't normally take and heard a familiar song play. It took him a few moments to realize it but it was "Amazing Grace." He had no idea it was Sunday, he had just stumbled upon a chapel and there were inmates, even one or two with some serious gang tattoos standing and singing that song. That song! It touched his heart, the sound of it filled him with happiness, brought back memories of when he had been an eager and young churchgoer. He stood outside the door to the Chapel and for the five or six minutes it took to sing the song he felt transformed again. But soon the feeling went away and he walked away, immersing his spirit back into the harsh realities of a prison full of violent criminals.

The next day he was sitting at lunch and a man came in to the dining area with a suit on that he had never seen before. He seemed to be looking for someone, and when he saw Bill he walked up and gently set a pamphlet down. Bill picked it up and looked at it, it was a flyer with information on how to request to attend church. Before the man turned, Bill crumpled it up and threw it on the floor.

That was the last Bill had to do with the prison chapel or chaplain for a very long time. Years passed and it became time to apply for parole and Bill was turned down a number of times. Then it happened. His liver shut down. It was a strange experience. His skin had begun to turn yellow and he felt a pain under the right front part of his ribcage. Then he couldn't keep anything down-not food, not water, not anything. It seemed like it was going to be his time to die and one day he just passed out and guards had to carry him to the infirmary. The doctor told him he had a very small chance of living another few weeks and he asked for the chaplain to come and see him.

"Hello, I understand you wanted to speak to me." Said the aging pastor who arrived at his bedside.

"Yes, I think I'm going to die soon and I wanted to get last rites or whatever it is that allows me to go to heaven."

"I remember you. You came to watch a service from the hall one day. I thought you had no time for religion."

"Are you going to pray for me, or what?" Bill asked in his toughest death-bed voice.

"Yes, I can pray for you but I don't know if it would do you any good. Do you believe in God?"

"I used to, when I was younger."

"If you don't believe now there really is no point."

"What difference does it make? I thought Jesus could forgive anyone."

"Anyone who is truly sorry. - I don't know if that is your case. I'm not going to lie to you, Son."

"Well then your job is done. You can take off. Leave me damned to hell for all eternity. I don't fucking care!"

"Before I go, can you tell me why you were sent to prison?"

"I stole some money and a guy picked a fight with me over a girl."

"I understand this 'guy' who picked a fight with you died."

"Yes, that's true."

"What made you feel you were justified in taking a life?"

"He stole my girlfriend, and I was drunk. Even the prosecutor didn't call it murder. It was manslaughter."

"Do you understand it was wrong?" Bill started to get a little misty-eyed.

"I don't know. After my grandmother died-she was the one that raised me-I guess I just kind of stopped caring about anything."

"You didn't stop caring. You cared about your girlfriend so bad you fought for her. It was wrong, but you aren't a monster. And you called for me. And then I saw you, I saw a light in your eyes when that song was playing." The Pastor took out a small mp3 player and started it going. "This was the song."

"But what good would it do-what is the point for me to confess my sins? I'm going to die in a few days!" As he said 'days' the player started to play "Amazing Grace" and Bill began to cry. "I didn't ask for this shitty life."

"But you did what you did. I can see that you're sorry. Sometimes there aren't miracles, but if you confess to me I know you will go to heaven and at the very least you will feel peace before you go." Bill began to sob openly.

"I... I... don't want to die. I can't die! I'm only 28! I never had a chance."

"What you do with what God gives you is your chance." As the song came to an end, the pastor stopped the player. "Now pray with me..." He reached out and took Bill's hand as he lay all yellowed and weak in the infirmary bed. They prayed a solemn prayer and Bill closed his eyes and went on in prayer for a half an hour about all the things he had done wrong, all he was sorry for. When he was done he felt clean, felt purged. Then the Doctor came in.

"Bill, I don't know how they managed it, but we have an organ donor match that has a liver we can give you."

"What... what does that mean?"

"It means with a little luck we can save your life, Bill." As he said this, the Pastor grasped Bill's hand and shook it and whispered, "hallelujah!" to himself.

"Bill cleared his eyes of moisture and gripped the pastor's hand back. The operation was done at the University Hospital the next day and in a month Bill was healthy enough to go back to prison. He started out spending a lot of time studying the Bible with his new Pastor and went into an alcohol rehabilitation program. From the day of his prayer onwards he was changed. He began to study not just the Bible, but school texts and when the opportunity arose a tutor was assigned, and if he ever had one there was no evidence that he still had a learning disability. Over the next two years he worked through four years of schooling and when his sentence was finished he had his high school diploma. Even though his life span was greatly shortened, Bill somehow reached down inside of himself and brought back the joy and the positive attitude he had towards life that he hadn't known since he was twelve. Before he finally passed, Bill had gotten a Counselling Diploma and a diploma from a seminary and spent his remaining days working with youth at risk and he died at 51 an accomplished and happy man. Why God needed him to kill someone to discover his forgiveness he would never understand, and though God must have, he never completely forgave himself.

THE END

THE MEDITATOR

It had become a habit for Jack, ending his morning of work with a walk over to the Casino for a cup of coffee. Days he didn't work he still went down, there was something he liked about the mid-day crowd in the lounge: there were some real characters in there. First there was Audie, who had been named after the 1950's Cowboy Movie star. Everyone knew he was a little crazy but all the time he would surprise people by knowing something no one else did. Like the fact that for a long time people thought he couldn't read and then he would spout out a quote from the Bible that someone had on the tip of their tongue. He was about 60 years old and had a fair sized pot belly, probably due to the fact that no one in the 10 years he had been coming to that lounge had ever seen him consume anything but beer.

Then there was Rob. In his day, Jack had known a few people named Rob and by some quirk of fate it seemed that all of them were pathological liars. Some people might change a detail or two about a story or forget part of it and fill it in to the best of their knowledge, but Rob would completely fabricate nearly everything that came out of his mouth. The funny thing was that no one cared. A good deal of the time they actually enjoyed listening to the guy because he could spin a good yarn. He was the kind of guy who would do anything for a laugh.

One time Jack came in and sat next to Rob and they started talking and Rob said that Maria's boyfriend was all pissed off at him. When Jack asked why that was, though he had no particular interest in the answer that came out of him, Rob said that he had gotten a tattoo of Maria's name on his shoulder. Then he said to Jack that he had also put his name on his shoulder. Jack was intrigued, and looked forward to confronting Rob when he went to show these supposed tattoos and they weren't there. So Jack called 'bullshit' and Rob took off his coat, rolled up his sleeve and there was a fresh tattoo, which read "your name" in blue ink. Jack looked at him blank-faced. The stupidity of this man, he thought to himself, knows no bounds.

    Jack was a fairly honest guy but he never really seemed to find many honest friends. He liked having people around to talk to, though, and he liked to feign interest and fake caring about other's lives when in reality it didn't add up to dried shit in his preferred version of reality. Paying the rent, having enough for food and video rentals was about it. He had quit smoking some years back, quit drinking some time after, and now had very few needs. Clothes maybe in the winter, nothing fancy because he worked unloading trucks. Just warm stuff and the odd set of gloves or a new pair of boots every couple of years. He didn't want a car and didn't really need much. Life went on like this for most of his 30's.

Jack reached the age of 37 and after having some cake with his aunt and cousin, his only surviving relatives, he got to thinking about a lot of things. Though he didn't have the sex drive of a teenager, he wouldn't mind getting together with a nice looking girlfriend. He even thought that he wouldn't mind having a kid at some point, but he also thought that he was getting a little over the hill, thinking that when the kid was 11 and needed a father to teach him to shave, how to shine a pair of shoes, how to toss a football, he would be getting to be an old crone. Still, there was time, just not lots of it.

One of the things that made him think was that he spent most of his time in a bar. He went there just about every day, drank coffee and had lunch, made sure to tip well and all but he wouldn't want to raise a kid with any of the women he knew that hung out there. There were just a few types of women who came to that bar, there were the hookers looking to latch onto some of the big spenders or even better, the guys that won a big pot in the Casino part of the building and came to the lounge to celebrate. Then there were the gamblers, the women who would sit at the Video Poker terminals and stuff in $20 bill after $20 bill and feel somehow superior because they weren't wasting their time at the blackjack tables. There was the odd young woman just come for a drink, but that was what they were, young women. Nice to look at but not ready to settle down or willing to settle down with a 37 year-old laborer. Then there were the odd female alcoholics, who would be living with or at least sleeping with one of the regulars at some point. None of them would make a decent life partner, but this was all Jack knew. These were his friends. There had to be a better way, and it wasn't to be found in going after waitresses.

Jack put a lot of thought into it and he realized he would have to change his playground if he wanted to change his playmates, or find a playmate. One of the things he figured would be good would be to get to a gym, or a pool, some place where people go on a regular basis like the bar. He decided to go all in and forked out enough for a swim and gym pass through the city. This he figured was the best thing he could do, because he could work out and look better, feel better and maybe meet someone with the same desires.

Each day for a few weeks, Jack would take the bus to the pool. He started spending more and more time there, swimming laps and then sitting in the sauna until sweat ran out of all of his pores, then jumping into the cool and refreshing water. He didn't know much about working out or swimming, but he knew it felt good. Then one day it happened: a small event that would turn the tide of his life.

Jack had swam more laps than normal, and felt a little dazed when he climbed up the underwater steps to the pool deck. He went to the shower outside of the sauna and set the water to cold and felt the icy blast run down his head and then all over him. He wanted to be icy cold and shivering when he went into the sauna, prolong the time he would be in there, until he felt completely cooked. It was a great feeling and it was also so he heard a great way to improve circulation. When he couldn't stand the cold anymore he shut off the shower and entered the comforting heat of the sauna. There was one person in there already: he looked to be Chinese. Jack had a funny feeling of familiarity when he saw him but he was fairly sure the man hadn't been at the pool while he had been coming.

"Afternoon!" Jack said in a friendly voice. The man nodded his head but said nothing.

Jack just assumed he didn't want to be bothered so he didn't say anymore to him. The man seemed to be concentrating, waiting for something. Sure enough, he took a long, deep breath, then folded his legs in a meditational type position and closed his eyes. Jack could see the perspiration forming on him knowing he had been in the sauna for some time and it seemed kind of fascinating. Jack sat down normally and closed his eyes, savoring the warmth, leaning his head back against the wood of the sauna walls. He got a little bored after a few minutes and looked down at his feet. He saw that one of his toenails was growing in kind of funny so he leaned over, and was able to bend it and tear it off because it had grown soft in the water and the heat. Not thinking, he flicked it and it landed on the rocks of the sauna and started to send up smoke that was absolutely acrid. Jack tried to pretend he didn't do it but the Chinese guy opened his eyes and the smell was horrible and he gave Jack a dirty look. Jack tried to smile but felt stupid so he left the sauna, dove into the water and swam to the other end of the pool and went to change and go home.

The next day Jack returned around the same time and he noticed the Meditator was there again. He was in the sauna but hadn't closed his eyes yet and wasn't cross-legged or anything, so Jack went in to talk to him.

"Sorry about the rocks yesterday." Jack said in a humorous tone of voice. "I had a temporary brain fart."

"What did you put on those rocks? That reeked!" The man said, seeming a bit put out. Jack was surprised that the man spoke perfect English and had no accent. He was expecting a Chinese voice. The man's speech was disarming.

"Oh, just a small piece of toenail that was coming off. I flicked it and it kind of went wide and landed on the rocks." Jack answered.

"Would you like to try meditating in here with me instead of driving me out of this relaxing room?" The Chinese man said.

"I'll try it. I'll try anything once. What all does it do?"

"Meditation lets us focus, lets the mind clear and as the toxins leave our body with the heat, the toxins leave our minds with the meditation." Jack thought it was odd that he seemed so kind and peaceful when he had such a mean look yesterday.

"Sounds great. How does it work? Does it take long to learn?"

"It can take a lifetime or it can take a moment. It depends on the heart, not the calendar. First you cross your legs and balance yourself." As he said this, he pulled in each of his legs under him. "Then you simply try to think of nothing. No clutter, no to-do list, just breathe. Count to ten, one number with each breath. If you think too much, go back to one. Then you keep going until you can get to ten."

"Sounds pretty good. I'll give it a try." Jack said, pulling his legs under him. His thick and muscled legs didn't get all the way under him, and his instructor laughed and said just to go as far as he could. He did so and then closed his eyes. It was kind of boring at first, but after a couple of breaths and starting over he realized it was going to be harder than he thought. After five minutes he opened his eyes and waited for his new friend to open his eyes. It took nearly 20 minutes and in that time Jack felt cooked.

"How long did you last?" The man queried.

"About five minutes." Jack said with a chuckle.

"That's good, very good for your first time. Try to practice every day, you will start to feel your mind get clearer." Came the kind-sounding reply.

"What's your name, friend?" Jack asked.

"My Chinese name is Chung, but my friends call me Charlie."

"Nice to make the acquaintance." Jack replied.

"Same time tomorrow?" Charlie asked.

"Same time. See you then." Jack was absolutely deep fried as he said this and made a hasty exit, jumping into the cold pool as soon as he could and paddling himself completely under water until he felt half human again.

That day Jack started to think about having a coffee and decided to stop by the lounge at the Casino and say hello to his friends there. He took the bus, then went inside and none of them had gotten there yet. He had his coffee and then wanted to stretch his tired legs so he took a walk through the Casino floor. By some odd chance Charlie was there wearing a tuxedo. He was a pit boss apparently. That was where he had seen him before Jack realized. He had seen the guy kick a guy out for whatever reason and Charlie apparently had gone through some pretty rigorous martial arts training, he kicked the guy's ass pretty good. He hadn't done it in years, but Jack decided for some reason he was going to sit down and play a little roulette. He pulled out a couple of $20 bills and put them down on the table and got some pink markers for them. He spread about $5 worth of chips around and when the ball stopped rolling one of his chips hit, giving him around $30 worth of chips. He sat back, raked in his chips and then made small bets and watched the ball spin closely.

For some reason the ball seemed to be favoring the high numbers, the upper 12 as they are known in some circles. He put down some chips on the upper third betting space on the outside of the marked portion of the green table and the first third came up. He doubled his bet next time, on the upper third again and it came in. another $40 in his coffers. His head started working faster, his eyes were darting around the board. He made a few more bets and some other players came and a small betting crowd seemed to gather. Things got too confusing so Jack stopped and cashed his chips in and went to the cashier. He ended up about $100 better off than when he came in, not too bad considering he didn't make a lot more than that in a day's work. He knew he was lucky though and luck never lasted.

Over the next few weeks Jack went on going to the pool and learning from Charlie how to meditate and things seemed to be going really well. Still, he often missed his friends at the lounge and the atmosphere of music and clean surroundings, so he still stopped in for a coffee and a meal quite often. One day he came in and when he went to sit down at his favorite chair he noticed a full cup of coffee there. He asked Gavin the bartender if someone had taken his spot but he told Jack that the lady by the window had bought it for him. He looked over and there was a very attractive Asian lady sipping at a girlie drink. He tipped the coffee cup to her, and she waved him over. His heart nearly skipped a beat, and when he went to go to her table he nearly shook so much he spilled his coffee, but she smiled at him and he somehow was able to take it in stride.

"Hi there, I'm Jack. Pleased to meet you, thanks for the coffee. How did you know I was coming now?"

"I am friend of Cha-Lee. I see you play, you very lucky. I tell Cha-Lee you handsome, he tell me you be here." You remember me?

"Oh yes, you were the roulette spinner. I don't remember you being so pretty." The lady smiled and waved her hand at him.

"My clothes pretty, work clothes not pretty." Jack smiled and looked in her eyes.

"So what did you wave me over here for?" Jack asked her.

The attractive female spinner slid a paper envelope over to him and said, "Look when I leave, then tear up. You come see me today." Then she took a final sip of her drink and nervously got up and left by the patio exit.

When she was gone, Jack opened the envelope and it read:

Use the ATM card inside to take $1,000.00

ATM code is 7777

Come to table #54 at 5:00pm

Get $100 value markers

Play the outside, alternate bets

Keep an eye on Charlie

When he coughs, put maximum $500 on #5

Take half, deposit rest in ATM

"Oh my God." Jack whispered to himself. Charlie you beautiful bastard. $500 on the inside is 36 to one, that's $18 grand, $9 for me. He looked up at the clock, it read 11:13 am. Trip to the bank and back, nice meal. Hang out here then... easy street. What the hell am I going to do with nine thousand bucks? A car. No. No. A condo. A nice little townhouse, rent the basement, have something to sell for retirement. Yes. Perfect. The clock ticked away, second by slowing second.

Jack sat and finished his coffee, though later he wished he hadn't. The caffeine had the effect of making his hands tremble and that made him think he was easy to spot as a con artist, which made him worry right down to the pit of his stomach. Then he started to feel guilty. But he turned off the moral side of himself and turned on the logical side. Who really loses here? He asked himself. The Casino? Those places are so crooked they are lucky no one has burned them down out of spite. I've been going in there, buying coffee, buying meals. Not the greatest meals either, their only good item on the menu is hamburgers and I've eaten enough of those to reimburse the $9k right there. No chance I'm passing this up.

Jack continued this self talk as he walked. For a few moments he felt a little paranoid, wondering if people were watching him, wondering who would see what in the Casino. Little did he know that almost nothing that happens in the Casino unless it's in the bathroom goes on without being seen. He got the cash, then went out for a steak and baked potato and a cold beer to calm his nerves. When he got back to the Casino, it was only 2:00pm and all the regulars were there. Happily, but without explanation he bought drinks for all his friends and had a few more himself. He really liked the feeling of a few drinks added to how much better he felt from working out. Time started to slip past, and he was a bit unsteady when time came to sit down at table #54. At first there wasn't room but he pushed his way through to the table and put down the $800 he had left, only he asked for $50 chips instead of $100. He felt invincible and thought if he made a few bets he would be even more ahead when the #5 bet came in and then he could really party.

It was just ten minutes to five and Jack decided to try his old trick that had never failed him before. He watched and waited, trying to figure out a pattern and he noticed the low 12 was coming up a lot. He put down two $50 chips on the low 12 and watched the metal ball roll across the 36 numbers and two zeros and land on 32..high twelve. He watched and waited again as the second twelve then the third twelve then the second twelve came up. Then he put $200 on the first 12, thinking it was due to pay. He watched the spinner wave her hand and declare, "no more bets" and the ball seemed to roll for eons as he waited for it to stop. Second 12, number 17 came up.

"Damn!" Jack said, and the small part of him that was still sober knew bad things could happen if this got screwed up. He took his remaining $500 and played the safest bet he could, black. Any number, 18 of the thirty-six could come up and if it were black he would be fine. He started to feel a little dizzy but this seemed like the right thing to do. The ball rolled, the hand waved, the lady spoke. The ball rolled. The ball rolled. Black, 25! The lady announced. For a minute he thought he had bet on the first 12 and didn't realize he just doubled back up to where he was. The chip counter pushed a stack of $50 chips over to his stack of 10 of them. He looked over at Charlie, who was actually sweating and he was coughing so hard he nearly doubled over. He looked at the roller, the Asian lady who had given him the envelope. She gave him a slight nod. Now he was sober. Dead sober. He had a little idea, a very little idea but it wasn't all bad.

"Pit boss!" He yelled. Charlie came over.

"Yes Sir?" Charlie replied.

"What's the maximum bet on the inside 36 numbers?" Charlie's eyes seemed to bulge. For some reason it looked as though he was actually angry for some reason.

"$500 at this table, Sir" Charlie said, gritting his teeth.

"I want to bet a thousand. Can I get approval?"

"Let me ask my boss, just one second." Charlie got on his radio and spoke a few words in Chinese and a few words came back. "Yes, Sir! You can bet a thousand."

"Okay, a thousand on #5." The spinner shot a quick glance at Charlie but he was too busy biting his tongue to see it. Jack slid the 20 $50 chips over and a couple of people put a lucky chip marker on top of it. The wheel spun and rolled and bobbled, and jumped around and finally came to rest on #5. The crowd that had been watching cheered, and a massive adrenalin rush went through Jack's whole body. The table didn't even have enough chips in his color to pay the bet, but Jack told them to cash him out and they gave him 72 $500 chips in payment. Then he went to the cashier and asked for two checks to be written which he filled in all but the name on both. Anyone watching might rob him but not knowing he didn't have the names wasn't apparent to anyone so he was reasonably safe. He put them both in envelopes, sealed them up and wrote "Pit Boss" on one and "Kathy" on the other, then he went out, deposited the "Pit Boss" envelope in the ATM then went for a long walk.

Jack walked for hours, for so long that the sun ended up coming up. He had felt good, and he had been a little drunk, which he hadn't been in a very long time but something weighed heavily on his heart. He walked and walked and then came to a little house with a beat-up old Chevrolet station wagon parked in the driveway and no lights on. He waited until the occupants woke up and after a while a young woman and a ten year-old girl came out. He was standing at the end of her sidewalk.

"Jack," the woman said. "I thought you were going to stay away from us. I thought we went over this."

"Jenny, I just wanted to give a little gift to my daughter."

"Mommy, who is this guy?" the little girl asked, confused.

"He's someone Mommy knew before you were born."

"Is he my Daddy?" she asked.

"No honey. To be a Daddy you have to work hard and provide and love and care for. This man never loved anything or gave anything or did anything."

"I don't understand Mommy." The little girl said, feeling afraid.

"I don't understand either. I don't understand why he is HERE!" The woman said, getting angry.

"Just take this. Take this envelope and I'll stay away forever."

"Put it in the mailbox. I have to take Kathy to school."

Jack felt a thousand pent-up emotions try to burst open his chest. His eyes began to tear up, but he solemnly walked to the mailbox and put the letter in it. Kathy and her Mother left and he stood there for a while, wondering what to do next, wondering if he should find a high bridge or a piece of rope or a fast moving bus to step in front of. Instead, he walked five miles to get back downtown and got on a bus headed East and he didn't get off it until it was near the Ocean where he got a job and a pair of boots and forgot about all that he left behind. He even found another bar but gave up swimming, except in the Ocean.

THE END

A LITTLE BLING, A LITTLE BOURBON

It was a typical winter's day in downtown Vancouver. The sky was drizzling a cooling rain and the sun only came out sporadically, just enough to remind the residents of the harbour city that they were in the warmest metropolis in Canada. Being the warmest metropolis in Canada was nice, but it was sort of like getting ice cream in February. You appreciated it, but it wasn't that big of a deal.

Frank Harper worked in renovation construction in the city of Vancouver, for a small company that he had gotten in touch with through a temp labour office. The temp office was a good place to go when you were down and out and needed a few days' work to get you through to something else, but Frank had been at this job now for 2 months and he was starting to get tired of it.

His job on this particular Tuesday afternoon was to take a sledge hammer and smash up a concrete floor in a bathroom, and when he was done, carry out the rocky chunks. It was back-breaking work at times and he also knew when he was done he would have to lug out the excruciatingly heavy radiator for the suite he was working in, so he was trying to take as much time as he could so he could go home before having to undertake this task.

Frank was a fit young man of 20 with muscular shoulders and a happy smile for just about anyone he ran across. He had red hair and blue eyes and a handsomeness to him that made people want to be around him, male and female. His core belief in life was that everyone was a good friend once you had a few drinks with them, and since he had gotten this job he had sat down for drinks with most of the guys on the crew, including his boss. He was relieved when he was near to finishing smashing up the floor that his boss Sheldon came in and motioned for him to stop working.

"Frank, got something for you. You can finish that floor later." Frank put down his sledge hammer and wiped his sweating brow as he followed the directional indication Sheldon was giving him with his index finger. It took the two men outside and around the west side of the apartment building.

"You see that board there on the side of the building?" Sheldon pointed at a piece of plywood that had been hammered over a hole in the outside wall of the soon to be extra ritzy walk-up apartment building.

"Yeah, what about it?" Frank asked.

"Here, take this hammer," Sheldon said, handing him a claw hammer, "and pull out the nails. There is a crawl space behind it. I need you to go see if you can find a leak in the plumbing at the end of it. You're the smallest guy on the crew so it has to be you. Sorry bud."

Frank never let anyone give him too much ribbing about his height, it had made him quite a scrapper in his younger days, but it was simple truth that the other 4 guys in the crew were middle aged and fat, so without too much grumbling, he removed the nails one by one from the plank. As he was leaving, Sheldon said to him,

"It will be easy to find the leak if it's there, you won't miss the smell. Don't lose those nails either, you need to hammer that plywood back on when you're done or that crawlspace will be crawling with homeless people by tomorrow." Frank waved acknowledgement and worked away at the wood covering. It didn't take him long to remove it and then he slipped in, easily guiding his lithe form down the crawlspace which was flooring above him and just dirt below.

Frank got to the end of the space and he could definitely smell something and it was pretty putrid. The leaking pipe must be from some kind of non-functioning toilet he thought because it was the most ripe odor he could imagine. The only way he could describe it would be to call it the stench of death. He didn't have a flashlight and the space was dark so he had to feel around for the leaking pipe. He put his hand into something wet and then smelled his hand and he knew he had found the cheesy smelling culprit. Above him Sheldon had gone back into the building and was in the suite where the pipe originated. He yelled down for Frank to hit the pipe with his hammer, which he did. Then all hell broke loose. Frank had hit the pipe with the claw hammer he had brought with him and it burst open right in front of him, spewing human waste all over his upper body, including his face. Frank let out a string of obscenities that would make a sailor blush and he could hear the other guys on the crew above him falling over themselves laughing. Fuck! He thought, those bastards think this is funny! He started to crawl backwards and get out of the stinking mess and he put his foot out to turn around and it knocked on something, something hollow.

While his co-workers were still in the grips of merriment, Frank dug out the box that his foot had hit and out of curiosity opened it. He didn't really know what to think at first, but inside was some kind of necklace. Then he took out his lighter and lit up the object and saw that it was either a really nice handcrafted rhinestone necklace or something really valuable. He slipped it into his pocket, returned the box to where he found it and crawled out. When he got out of the hole and walked around to the building there were his 'friends' ready to deal with a young man as angry as a castrated bull. But to their surprise, he was calm and composed, and Frank didn't say anything to them though except to ask Sheldon if he could go home early to take a shower. Sheldon agreed and Frank left, smelling worse than rotting ground beef with stains all over his clothes. It was all his co-workers could do just to keep from laughing.

Frank decided to walk that day. He knew he smelled bad, the stink came out of his clothes and his face felt greasy. He couldn't face the looks he would get if he took the bus. The only small solace he had was that the rain helped clean off a bit of his skin. Frank now had a reason to keep his calm though. He had a little errand to run.

It was a long walk, but Frank made it to Hastings Street and looked for the seediest pawn shop he could find. He went in to a shop called "Honest Abe's", and a raggedy looking older man wearing a stove-pipe hat with what was most likely a fake Abraham Lincoln beard stood behind the counter.

"How can I help you young man?" The caricature figure asked.

"I need to find out if this is worth something." Frank pulled the necklace out of his pocket and set it down on the counter. Honest Abe got out a magnifying glass and had a close look, though you could see his nose twitch from the moment he picked up the jewelry.

"What do you want to do with it?" He asked. Frank noticed that as he was looking at something on the back of the necklace, he raised an eyebrow. That was his only indication it was worth anything.

"I want to sell it of course, it was my mom's." Frank said, lying. "She passed away." He added, hoping to cement the effect of his ruse.

"And what is it worth to you?" Abe asked, raising an eyebrow again only this time sizing up his customer rather than the item.

"Twelve Hundred." Frank said, feeling a bit nervous and silly standing in front of this clown. He didn't know if the thing was worth twelve cents.

"I'll need identification." Frank let out a long sigh. His gamble-bid of twelve hundred dollars was a good one. His nervousness was now edged with elation.

"Sorry, don't have any ID." Frank lied again.

Honest Abe set the necklace down, then turned around to see if anyone else in the store was watching. "No ID, I'll give you a thousand, but don't think you can come back any time and ask for more. A thousand, final sale."

"Deal." Frank said, and he watched as Honest Abe put the necklace into his floor safe and came out with ten new hundred dollar bills. Frank grabbed them and rushed out. Just as he did, Honest Abe took out a spray bottle and fumigated the unique presence Frank had brought with him right out of his store.

Frank rushed home, but made one stop to pick up a 40 ounce bottle of fine bourbon on the way. Him and his roommate were going to get nice and loaded thanks to some random person that possibly wasn't even alive anymore. He got inside and the first thing his roommate said was,

"Holy shit man, what happened to you?"

"Never mind dude, here, take this and get started. I gotta jump in the shower." He handed over the bottle.

"You need to throw out those clothes too man and consider a new deodorant."

"Yeah, and I also need to get drunk tonight. Are you in or not?"

"I'm in, I'm in!" Franks' roommate Glen said as he opened the bottle and went for glasses. "Hey-how the hell did you get the good stuff? I thought you were broke."

"I'll tell you in a minute." Right away, Frank started stripping off his clothes which he stuffed into a garbage bag he got from the kitchen. He took his money and stashed it in his drawer and went into the bathroom. The smell that had been splashed all over him from that old pipe was so vile he could hardly imagine that he had made it this far with it. Out of curiosity he stuck his face in the garbage bag with his clothes in it and when he breathed in he literally threw up. Luckily his face was already in the bag, but unlucky for his clothes. At first he thought he could maybe wash them but now he didn't think he ever wanted to see them again. He tied up the bag and tossed it in the kitchen and dashed back to a soothing hot shower. Frank showered for a good half hour and when he was done Glen had already taken the bag of shit clothes to the garbage. He changed into fresh jeans and a t-shirt and came out to see that Glen had gotten a good head start on him with the bourbon.

The next three days were a non-stop party. They ordered booze delivered, they went to bars and tried to pick up women. They bought hash and shared it with anyone who had the need. They didn't sleep, they barely ate, and when they felt the party was winding down they popped pills and dropped hits of LSD they got from a stoner friend that lived in their building. As the end of the money was coming, Glen finally asked:

"Dude, when are you going to tell me where you got this money from?"

"Well, I guess I can tell you since you got the benefit of it. I found a necklace and pawned it."

"Where did you pawn it?" Glen asked.

"Honest Abe's on Hastings. He did it for me under the table." Frank smiled and said, "gave me a cool thousand for it, thing didn't cost me a cent." Glen suddenly looked like he had just been told he was HIV positive.

"Dude, they're going to catch you! Someone's going to miss that thing and they'll catch you! If this Honest Abe dude gave you a thousand it's probably worth a lot more. You need to turn yourself in." Frank looked at Glen while he said this and couldn't help but think he was a little bit crazy. He seemed to be making sense but he was tripping Frank out big time. .

"Turn myself in? You come up with this idea now? We blew the money, I can't turn myself in. Besides, no one knows about it."

"Dude, they have cameras in these places! They have cameras on Hastings! They'll find you." Frank saw a look of fear and confusion well up in Glen's face. Frank himself was hung over and coming off hash and maybe some other stuff he didn't know he had taken likely mixed in just for fun. The fact was though, that Glen was really starting to piss him off.

"Cameras? Glen man, get your head straight, everything will be fine. Why don't you have a beer or two, take the edge off."

"No man, something bad is gonna happen. The police are going to find us. They have the alien technology that can track us down through the fillings in our teeth! Why do you think they take x-rays every time you go to the dentist?"

"Fuck Glen, calm down! You're freaking me out!" He yelled. Frank didn't know how to react to this strange behavior. He sure as hell wasn't going to go along with him.

"No, I have to call the police, it's the only way." He spoke as though he were a man with a sacred mission. He got up and started to walk towards the phone. Frank grabbed him and they struggled. Glen made it to the phone and was dialing something and Frank just lost it. He pummelled Glen with punches, his strong and muscled arm pounding Glen's head again and again. Glen started screaming and Frank hit harder and started screaming himself. Then Frank blacked out and when he could think again Glen lay there in a pool of his own blood, not moving, not breathing. Soon as he sat drinking, propped up against a wall, tears forming in his eyes he could hear sirens drawing closer. Then he heard footsteps from two directions and then yelling and a heavy boot crashing into his door. Frank just sat there until he was carted off to jail.

The trial didn't take long. Frank pleaded not guilty to manslaughter and was convicted and given fifteen years. The first prison he was sent to was Kingston Penitentiary, the oldest and the most feared prison in the Canadian system. As he sat in his cell day after day, month after month, year upon year, he always thought it was odd how just in behind the scent of the second rate cleaning products they used in that prison was the unforgettable odor that he had known that day when he found the necklace. It still made him gag a bit in the mornings when he would smell it for the first time each day.

Frank didn't fare well in prison after he had been there a while. The details of what is done to young men doing hard time are well known, and, as he did his time, violence begat violence and he eventually was tagged a dangerous offender, to be incarcerated for life. At first he took his beatings and gang rapes and just tried to do his time, but the thing that seemed to turn him into a true prison badass was when he was reading the newspaper and ran across an article of interest:

Toronto Man Strikes It Rich Once More!

Self-made millionaire Bill Janse has once again shown that it takes money to make money. And he has made a lot of it. Mr. Janse was on a recent trip to Vancouver where he purchased an item for his wife for five thousand dollars that he thought was an ordinary diamond necklace. As it turns out, this necklace was hand-made by a world-class jeweler for Queen Elizabeth on the occasion of her coronation, and was missing since the 1950's from the jeweler's studio

Janse was told this information when he went

to get the piece appraised, and turned in the incredibly

rare necklace and was given a reward Of $120,000.00

for his honesty, a tidy profit.

    Above the article was a picture of the necklace Frank had found many years back on what he had right then and there decided was the shittiest day of his life.

THE END

Leif Gregersen

NIGHT FLIGHT OVER FORTRESS EUROPE

It was a chilly summer night at the Southern England Air Base in July of 1942. Frank Hereford sat in his private quarters, reading over the specifications and other information with regards to the new Spitfire mark ix he was going to fly at any given moment. He was waiting to be given orders and though he had a good idea of what they were going to be, secrecy had to be kept until the very last moment.

Flying was a game Frank knew well, he had been at it for fifteen of his 35 years. Wealthy parents and a lust to navigate the skies allowed him to pursue his goal of being a top-notch pilot when most people in England were lining up for soup or other handouts. It was not a fair system, but now that most of those soup-eaters were able to keep two feet on the ground and live in relative safety compared to him, flying missions all over Europe, his life at the mercy of his own skill versus that of the enemy, he felt as though justice had been served.

Commander Hereford was actually quite pleased at the specifications about the new Spit, it looked like it could fly faster and turn quicker than the ME109 and even the German's newer plane, the FW190. He was a bit ticked off that there would be no chance for him to test fly the plane, he was simply given manuals and expected to react to flying it as if he had been flying it all along. This was something that could get dangerous, especially if aerial combat was a possibility.

As he was admiring the new plane and mentally going through what it would be like to pull a fast turn on a German plane and move in for the kill in it, a knock came at the door. He had known it would be coming, but he would have much rather been sleeping the night away and waking up next to his wife than having to fly another mission. His stomach tightened and he felt the taste of bile in his throat, despite the fact that, with his experience, he was possibly the most deadly ace in England.

"Commander Hereford Sir?" Came the voice with the knock.

Frank opened the door to see Thompson, one of the brighter young LAC's he had taken up in two-seaters and had more than once thought of recommending for flight training. They said he was too young and hadn't completed his secondary school so Britain would have to pass on another candidate for the one big thing they lacked: pilots.

"Yes Thompson, what is it?" He said in a bit of an annoyed tone. He knew he was going to be summoned but this was his own way of sounding off that he didn't like being chosen for these tricky assignments that always turned out to be dangerous. It didn't do him any good, but it often kept people edgy when they were around him, especially the lower ranks, which he liked to do. To him, this was one of the God-given privileges that officers had over lower ranks.

"I have orders for you Sir, from the Squadron Leader." Thompson replied, being careful not to let on that the Commander made him nervous.

"Very well, very well, give them to me and don't stand there like I'm going to tip you."

"Sorry Sir, my instructions are to give you the orders and watch you destroy them."

"I suppose burning would be good enough."

"That would be what was intended in the order Sir."

"Well, I don't smoke man. What am I supposed to do, eat them?"

Thompson handed Commander Hereford his own lighter and took a step back from the door without closing it. The orders read as follows:

COMMANDER HEREFORD, EYES ONLY.

YOU ARE TO TAKE THE NEW SPITFIRE MARK IX

FLY IT TO THE AREA MARKED ON THE MAP

SEEK OUT THE STRUCTURE DRAWN BELOW

TAKE AS MANY PICTURES AS YOU CAN OF IT

THEN RETURN TO BASE IN A CIRCUITOUS ROUTE

YOU ARE NOT TO ENGAGE THE ENEMY

UNLESS YOU ARE FORCED TO

Commander Hereford took a long look at the map and then set flame to both documents. He made sure they burned completely and put them into an empty waste basket. Then he dismissed Thompson and made his way to the pilot's locker room to get into his flight gear.

Hereford knew what they were after. Many planes and lives had been lost going after the same thing. The Germans had been making rockets, and if they were allowed to complete their plans the entire balance of power could be easily changed between the Allies and Axis powers. Once he got his gear in order he made his way to the intelligence building and had a long chat with his friend Archie about German anti-aircraft emplacements and the various airfields that could be alerted to his presence. He had become one of the top pilots in the RAF by his incredible memory and devotion to every detail of each mission, not to mention his skill and marksmanship. This had also made him part of an even smaller class of men, one of the top live pilots in the RAF.

Soon after his all-too brief briefing, he had climbed into the cockpit of the new Spitfire and was quickly told what to expect once he got the plane in the air and how the camera worked. With a crisp salute and smile, Frank was taxiing down the runway to a new adventure he really wished he could have let someone else experience.

It felt good, it felt renewing to push the throttle handle forward and guide the aircraft's tail up, then cautiously lift it off the main wheels and take to the air, retracting the wheels for greater speed and lift and freeing itself from all the bounds of the Earth. This was the part of flying Frank loved the most, before he had spent all his effort and skill on the completion of a mission, before his plane was shot up and nearly out of gas or the wheels were leaking hydraulic fluid forcing him to land belly-up. He decided he was going to fly south west until he hit Cornwall and then lower his altitude greatly and try to sneak past any German patrols by roughly following the outline of France over the water. A more direct route would take him over Normandy where a plethora of German airborne and land-based defenses would almost surely pepper him with everything they had. Those were the facts though, most of the missions he and his squadron mates were sent on were out over that area, and any pictures or intelligence achieved was like Gold. Both the Germans and the Allies wanted to find out as much as they could about the Normandy and surrounding coastal area, because soon there would have to be an invasion. Little did they know that the invasion would be useless if the rocket building areas and launches weren't kept in check or, with any luck, destroyed.

Out over the water a million stars shone above him and the moon was just over the horizon. It looked so huge there and it sent out a lot of soft yellow light. It was risky to send a mission at this time when the moon was full, but the planners back home had hoped the extra light could possibly illuminate a target that he would be photographing. He could take pictures in the dark, but as far as finding something worth taking picture of, that was another problem. This was an incredibly important, super-secret mission, but it was also incredibly dangerous and most likely useless. He had flown these 'rocket-finding' missions before and he had yet to see anything but the enemy aircraft he was forced to destroy. Frank had likely shot down more than 30 enemy planes, but he wasn't decorated or even recognized as doing so because it was so important to keep his missions quiet.

After a little more than an hour or flying out over the water, Commander Hereford turned his lithe and powerful Spitfire into land and headed to some industrial and farm country to the south of Bordeaux. He mentally calculated, with the help of the instrument cluster in the Spit how long it would take for him to check out the area in question. Then, he took his altitude down to tree-top level in hopes that he could evade more threats in that way. Certainly lower level flights would avoid radar, but if this was a rocket site, it would most likely give itself away by being doubly fortified with anti-aircraft guns and patrols of German fighters. As he drew in closer it seemed to him that this was just another falsely acquired piece of intelligence.

Frank neared the target and as he pulled back on the stick and gained altitude, he thought of his young wife who had hopefully long since gone to bed and what would happen if he didn't come home from a mission. He loved her dearly and they had hoped to have a child or two one day. It made him sick to think of raising a child when such brutality and destruction existed. Years back when the War started it seemed he was a thousand years younger, he was so eager to sign up, so full of piss and wind about how he and his squadron would fly to glory over Germany. The battle of Britain claimed the lived of 60% of his original squadron and most of the ones that survived that were lost in bomber escort missions. Over Germany. Even after all that, Frank had decided that he would personally give everything he could of himself to end the War or die trying, so he requested a transfer to intelligence and here he was. So many people had cheered on the aviators when the Battle of Britain ended. Fact was that when the sirens used to go off it was very common to see men vomiting from the incredible strain it took on them to fly two, three sorties a day facing down wave after wave of enemies, knowing that each time they failed to nail a bomber or fighter someone would die either in another aircraft or from having a bomb drop on them. He remembered landing after pitched battles, him and the other men counting the returning planes, hoping all of them made it, knowing that most of the free world was watching too.

Still, somehow as Frank was executing a climbing turn, keeping his eyes peeled at ever little abnormality or such as he checked out the area, still this was an enjoyable thing to do. The good feeling lasted for about 27 seconds. He was taking the last of the pictures he was going to take and he came around to spot two Me109's turning to engage him.

As a trick to see if they had spotted him, the Commander flipped his Spitfire over in a belly-up position, and dropped down to around 100 feet from the 1,500 feet he was taking photos from. It was harder to spot the plane upside down, though few pilots had the skill, it was a trick that often worked. This time it didn't.

One of the 109's was able to spot him and he left the second German plane to cover him while he dove after Frank's Spit. Frank flipped over and put the throttles to full and dropped down even lower. While he was gaining speed, the first 109 being in a dive, there was a brief moment when the enemy had him in his sights and the enemy took full advantage, pouring a staccato stream of 20mm cannon rounds from it's two nose cannon into Hereford's plane. Frank responded by pulling up, reducing throttle and putting the Spitfire into a sharp left-hand turn with 60% flaps. The Messerschmitt responded by diving down and trying to copy and outdo the Spitfire but the Me109's weren't nearly as good at turns as the Mark IX's. They went through a number of circles, and at the end of the third, Frank had the German dead to rights. He unleashed the power of his own guns and must have hit a fuel line because the plane exploded in the air, and the pilot had no chance to get out and use his chute.

    For a moment, Frank thought he was in the clear, but then he realized there had been two 109's. He closed his eyes for a moment and before he opened them, he once again heard the staccato rhythm of twin 20 mm cannons going off, ripping out most of his rudder, something he would need to return to England. Most pilots at this time would have opened up their canopy and jumped, but instead, Frank pulled back his stick and went straight up, where the enemy plane could hear him but hopefully not see him. He then completed the manoeuver by completing a loop and ended up right behind and above the German, and let loose on him until his right wing broke off, which actually took just seconds. In the reality of aerial combat though, mere seconds can be your life expectancy if you don't learn fast to hit hard and run. This time, the pilot got out and his parachute opened. This was another thing about the gallantry of the skies, which was being done less and less as this frightening war continued. If at all possible, a fighter pilot will take out the plane instead of the man.

/////////////////////////////

The kill was good. It actually had left Commander Hereford with an immense feeling of satisfaction. Unfortunately the fight had also left him without a portion of his tail rudder. He could still steer, the damaged control surface wasn't completely gone, and a plane actually didn't turn with just a rudder. He was going to have problems getting his damaged Spit back to England because he would only be able to make awkward turns and if there was a rough wind when he went to land, just using his ailerons was going to make things difficult. But Hereford had been through difficult landings before.

There had been one landing where he had just ounces of fuel left in his tanks and he was being pursued by a FW190, a nasty German plane for anyone to knock out of the sky. He wasn't far from his airfield, but he was leading this plane right to it's location where it would more than likely take out a number of targets before they could even leave the ground. Luckily though he was able to establish radio contact and let his boys know this plane was coming and that he would be in front of it, desperate to land. He streaked over the airfield and pulled up for altitude, which he would need for the landing, but in the eyes of the German pursuing him would be suicide, but as the German pulled up to move in for the kill, the full force of the airfield's anti-aircraft batteries let loose and annihilated the German plane. The pilot got out however, and despite a wound in his leg from the flak that downed him, he was an amiable sort. He was quite happy when he had heard that he would be sent to Canada as he had been fascinated more with the Democracy among plenty that the Country seemed to be about that he had for a long time wanted to go there. Hereford even sat him down while they were waiting for the Military Police to come and pick him up and drank most of a bottle of Johnny Walker Red label with him. For the German pilot the war was over, for Frank it was just beginning.

There wasn't going to be much hope of a rescue like that he had pulled over his own airfield with the amiable German though, his plan was to top out the plane's optimum altitude and speed capability and run hell for leather at over 400 mph at the altitude of 25,000 feet the manual had said was the plane's optimum. At that speed it could outrun just about anything in the sky. He strongly hoped the few things he couldn't outrun would be down for maintenance on that particular night.

Twice as he headed for home that night a German plane had spotted him and both times they simply had no way of keeping up with him, the Mark IX was just too fast. He was able to get on the radio and establish contact with an airfield just past the waters of the English channel, but as he neared the end of France over Normandy, he spotted an enemy squadron of bombers and fighters headed right at him, guns blazing, possibly alerted of his presence by spotters on the ground.

The Commander took a number of hits to his plane, leaving his engine coughing smoke and slowing his speed greatly. By a grand stroke of luck, a flight of American P-51 Mustangs had been sent up to pursue the bombers and fighters, and the fact that these German planes were now turning to try and down Commander Hereford was going to make the Mustang pilots' job much easier. One of the American pilots peeled away from the formation and took it upon himself to escort Frank back to the airfield he was headed for. "God bless those yanks." Frank said to himself. "Maybe one day I will even forgive them for being late in joining this bloody war."

Having lost most of his power, and a good bit of his maneuverability, Frank decided the best thing he could do would be to gain altitude. The Spitfire could glide quite a way on no power, and with a smoking engine that could catch fire at any time, the soonest possible chance he could get to shut off the engine would be the safest. Not to mention that he really didn't want to end up in the freezing waters of the English Channel, rescue boat on it's way or no. He climbed all he could, then when he had estimated he could come in to where the airfield was located and have a safety margin to over-fly the airport and get an idea of how it lay and which way the wind was blowing, he shut down the Rolls Royce engine that had brought him all this way and said a silent prayer to himself, the one he normally saved for roulette and cards.

As Frank sat there in the relative calm and silence of the still early morning sky over the Channel, a feeling of peace came over him. He remembered as a child what his brother would say when a peaceful, serene moment would come like this one, "I'm so relaxed I could shit." Funny how things like that come up. His brother had been in America after the previous war and had died in the flu pandemic that had killed at least as many people of the Great War. That was so long ago, yet there were times when Frank would reach for a sheet of stationary to write him a letter and in the reaching remember he was gone.

More important things than memories were pressing on his mind, as now he had glided down to 5,000 feet. The American plane had left him to his own devices now, leaving with a crisp salute and a victory roll, as the airfield was now coming into view. It looked like a rough and barely used field, with the odd wrecked truck or burned out plane near the runway. This could have been one of the earlier fields of the war, now abandoned except for skeleton staff that were there to help bring in damaged aircraft from missions gone wrong.

Although it looked like he had estimated the altitude he would need to glide in was wrong, the extra space he had allotted to check out the field would not be needed since he had gotten a visual confirmation so quickly as to where he would be setting down. He was coming in fast, feeling that he was going to hit hard if he tried to land at this speed, so he instinctively pulled back on the stick and slowed the Spitfire, which made it harder for him to keep the plane going in a straight and level forward motion. The controls of a plane in the cockpit can do three things, go up and down, with the use of the horizontal stabilizer in the tail, go left and right with the help of the tail rudder, which was now shot off, and roll right or left with the ailerons which are in the main wings.

   As Frank was trying to keep his plane going slow enough to safely touch down, he could only do two of these things. When you turn a plane, you need to co-ordinate the tail rudder, using your two foot pedals and the roll function which is done with the left-right movement of the control stick. You can turn with only the left-right movement of the stick, but it is awkward and extremely difficult to make a landing like that. This particular landing would be a rough one.

   There was no wind to speak of, which would work in Frank's favor, though his heart seemed to beat faster and faster with each yard he got closer to the runway. In one instance as he drew in he over-controlled and his plane went back and forth as he tried to right it and had to fight and unlearn how to turn with rudders. He lowered his flaps as he eased through 1,500 feet, which are the two 'flaps' of moveable control surface on the inside part of each wing. Lowering them meant turning a crank which kept them in one spot, causing air to move faster over the top of the inside of the wing and slower over the bottom, giving more lift at lower speeds. He had delayed this action to 1,500 feet because, though it made it easier to fly a slow-moving plane, it drew from the plane's inertia or 'forward-moving force' and this was something Frank was low on. He was slowing down just slightly too fast.

The seconds ticked by, Frank kept a close eye on the wind sock. A sudden gust could send him off course, and that would be a disaster at the least. He was tense everywhere, but then he remembered that he had done this in training and the real thing before, he relaxed his grip on the flight stick, took a deep breath and let himself fly by instinct. In he came, his main wheels touching down just at the edge of the runway. It was quite a bumpy ride, as this airfield seemed to have not been maintained in any special manner, but he did touch down. For seemingly no reason whatsoever, Commander Hereford laughed to himself, maybe because he had cheated the Gods one more time.

After his main wheels were down and he felt the aircraft was stable, he let down the tail section which had remained in the air for the first part of the landing as one must do with any 'tail dragger'. That was where the problem came in. When a small plane touches down, being at a higher speed, it is first kept moving in a straight line down the runway by ailerons, the main-wing control surfaces. As it slows, most such aircraft have brakes, which are at the tip of the rudder controls on the floor. Using his skill gained in training, you mainly guide the aircraft down the runway with rudders and brakes in the final part of the landing. When Frank slowed, he hit a bump or a stone on the right hand wheel and when he tried to recover instinctively, he turned and the speed of his plane caused it to tip. Now there was nothing he could do. He had sincerely hoped to bring this Spitfire back in one piece, as it had been nice enough to reciprocate for him. Now he had to deal with something every pilot fears, Fire!

His smoking engine must have been leaking fuel, which was ignited somehow in the flipping over. There was no rush of sirens, no emergency vehicles to come in and save him. He would have to get out on his own. He struggled with the canopy and it didn't want to budge under the strength of his arms or even his will. Frank Hereford was not a man to give up easy, so he turned himself upside down, took out his pistol and fired three shots at one of the thick canopy windows, then kicked at it for all he was worth. Somehow it popped out and he tried to exit the cockpit through the hole but had no luck. He decided he himself could fit but not his flight gear and clothing. He took out a knife from his pocket and, as the flames grew around him, he cut off what he couldn't struggle out of until he was stripped down to his long underwear. He then tried again and managed to squeeze out most of himself. Now, a jeep had arrived and came to help him try and escape the burning wreck. The two of them working together, got him out, though the flames and spitting oil did a good job on what was left of Frank's uniform.

The two of them scrambled away, knowing the plane could blow up at any minute. Then Frank and the Sergeant who had just saved his life sat on the grass, enjoying a brief respite from the insanity of the war. In around two more minutes, the Spitfire blew, and the two just watched, laughing at the fate that had brought the two away from the burning wreck just in time. The Sergeant, a Canadian offered a suggestion that they should get some sausages from the mess to cook over the fire.

"If it wasn't an oil fire, I would agree with you. Say, what normally happens when a pilot lands here at this time of night?"

"Well, I billet him in that building, " He said, pointing to a comfortable looking pre-fabricated structure. "Then in a day or two they send someone to get you."

"Two days eh! Any liquor about?"

"I keep a fair sized stash in my quarters, yes."

"Well then Sergeant, you and I are going to have a good time getting to know each other. Sometimes it seems I haven't had a good drink since this bloody war started."

"I know exactly how you feel Sir. I'll get you some coveralls from the mechanic's stores then we'll sit down by the wireless and toast the fact that we lived to fight another day."

"Sergeant, I get the feeling with a recommendation I'm going to make you're in for a medal and a promotion, maybe a posting away from this little lump of Earth."

"Promotion or no Sir, I'll still have to charge you for the booze, stuff is bleeding hard to get around here."

"Cheap bastard."

"It's the War Sir, it's the bloody War."

THE END

SMALL TOWNS, GOOD TIMES

Seventeen was a great time to be alive in Darren's home town of Wetaskawin late in the 1980's. He drove one of the coolest cars in his school: a 1972 Camaro in awesome shape. He had finally made a few cool friends and his best friend Doug was of the legal age to buy alcohol, which at the time was only 18. In just another year Darren would be able to head into Edmonton and cruise the bars and pubs for only the most delectable of women him and Doug could find.

On this particular night, a Friday, Darren and Doug were playing their favourite game, which they called 'quarters'. It was a well known drinking game on College and University Campuses. The way these two young men played it was there would be a glass on the kitchen table and they would try and bounce a quarter into it. If they got one in, the other guy had to take a drink, usually about a shot of beer. Before long they were pretty much guaranteed to be smashed out of their trees.

Doug lived in a small house with his parents who spent a lot of weekends in Edmonton, so his house was the place of choice for their drinking binges. Darren's home was quite a bit more strict than Doug's, though Darren's Dad likely drank a lot more booze than Doug's parents put together. His parents were always home, except for a rare time when they needed to leave, but they would make sure and bring their two boys, Darren and his brother Steve with them.

The other thing Darren's parents would do was to make sure he left his car keys behind when he went out on the weekend. They knew he drank a lot and that his driving skills weren't the best, which worried them what they would be like if he were drunk.

The two boys played their game for about two hours and polished off a 12 pack of beer and found that they were not as blasted as they wanted to be and had the teenager's curse of having little money between them. All of Darren's money from his car lot job went for gas and repairs to his car, and what allowance Doug got out of his Mom went for beer. It was sort of understood that as long as Doug continued to supply them both with beer, Darren would continue to drive him everywhere.

Together, rifling the pockets of his parent's coats and digging around for change brought up $12.00, just enough for another 12 pack at the one bar in town that sold alcohol after Alberta Liquor Control Board Hours. The only problem was the place was on the far side of town and the two of them, despite insistence to the contrary, were in no shape or mood to walk. Doug was the first to come up with a bright idea.

"Darren, man, see that 4x4 three-quarter ton truck down the block?" Doug said, pointing at the picture window that opened to the front street.

"Yeah, what about it?"

"It's been sitting there for a week. The guy who owns it is up in Fort MacMurray."

"So? Did you develop some lock-picking and hot-wiring skills that I don't know about?" Darren replied.

"No man, get this... I can see him come home every night from my bedroom, and I think I have him figured out. He uses one of those magnetic things to hide a spare key above the back left wheel. Fuck walking, man! Let's just borrow that thing for a quick run. He'll never know we did it."

"Yeah, but there's a problem." Said Darren, ever the straight man in this comedy duo. "I will know I did it, and if anyone else finds out and we get caught, the cops will know and then you and I will end up in jail."

"Jail? Jail!? Don't be such a pussy, man! They don't send kids like you to jail! Maybe a couple of months in the juvenile hall, nothing more."

"You want to go? Go ahead. Go get the beer, come back. What do you need me for?"

"It's a standard transmission."

"What? What's that supposed to mean?"

"I can't drive one."

"All this time I've known you. What is it, a year at least. You told me you had a Mustang Fastback with a three-speed in it. Ha! That's too funny. Were you always a pathological liar?"

"I had a car. I did have a car, but it was an automatic."

"What kind of car?" Darren said, feeling quite smug.

"A 1980 Chevy Citation." Doug said solemnly.

"Why couldn't you tell me that? Why couldn't you admit you couldn't drive a standard before this? I would have taught you."

"Well, I guess I was kind of jealous. You have these rich parents and you get a car and all that... You have a nice machine too. That car looks good on you. Flashy red paint job, spoiler and so on. I've always had to take a back seat to you rich people, and quite frankly it feels like shit."

"Look, Doug. You and me are like brothers. I've never had a friend like you, but I have to tell you my parent's didn't buy me that car. My dad signed for a loan for part of it but I had to go find a job. I had to make my own resume. I had to flip burgers for a year and a half until I got my present job."

"Your dad signed for the loan. And you don't see it. Don't you understand my dad could not and would not ever sign for a loan for me. And my dad doesn't have any friends who get me jobs, he doesn't even have a credit rating. I asked him why. You know what he said?"

"No, what?"

"He said if you can't afford it don't buy it. So here's Doug... all the other people at school have sweet rides. Some have new cars. What do I have? I have the choice of slaving my ass off and saving up for a $500 beater that dies 3 months later or I can just do without."

"Doug, man. I know life isn't fair. But in a couple of months we'll be graduating. You can go to Edmonton or Fort MacMurray or anywhere the money is good and in a few years no one is going to care who had a car and who didn't. I'm going to college. I don't have a choice in that matter. Not if I want to ever speak with my family again. I'd like to hop in the Camaro and take off up North, make some real cash and come back for school or even a business. Keep on getting drunk with you, keep on having friends who don't see me as a free ride or a competitor for some scholarship. I hate that academic shit but I'm good at it. So get this, man. I have to sell my fucking car just so I can take more boring classes until I'm totally institutionalized, only instead of being in jail I'll be in some high-rise going over the books of a half-assed pizza restaurant."

"Okay, okay. Enough already. Are we going for a beer run, or aren't we?"

"Fuck it." Darren said, having convinced himself. "We're going."

The two boys looked out the picture window at the street. In just seconds they went from being ordinary drunken teenagers to some kind of professional criminal. They 'cased' things out, walking by the truck, one of them giving it a good hard push to see if an alarm would go off and nothing happened. Doug went past first and felt around the wheel well for the magnetic key holder and got it on the first try. Then, he opened the driver's side door and got in, sliding over to the passenger side and then Darren came, a look of intensity on his face. Most normal people would be pretty drunk after six beers in two hours, but Darren had been practising and he was only slightly buzzed. Sober enough to drive but drunk enough to do perhaps the stupidest thing he had ever done in his life up to that point.

Darren put the key into the ignition and a long, starter-burning engine turning rung in his ears. He stopped, then turned it over again. Again, it turned over but didn't start.

"Shit!" was all he could think to say, though he kind of hoped this was the end of their little escapade.

"Give me two minutes. I think I know what's wrong." Doug got out of the truck, opened the hood and, standing on his tiptoes of the lift-kitted truck, he was able to feel around the engine until finally he got to the distributor cables, the middle one of which was unplugged. He would have to remember to unplug it again when he got back, he noted mentally. Then he gave a twirling sign with his hand and after just a couple of turns the engine roared to life. Doug got in and gave a quiet whoo-hoo just like the Dukes of Hazzard would have given, and Darren let out the clutch and tore off, just barely avoiding spinning his tires.

As they drove down the street, not going too fast, not going too slow, Darren asked Doug, "Dude, check the glove box for some smokes. I'm dying for one." Actually, at the rate his heart was pumping, nicotine was likely the last thing he needed, but Doug opened it up.

"I think I could use one too, buddy. They opened it up, and there was a flip-top pack of American cigs, a treat for any Canadian smoker. Doug opened it up, pulled out two smokes, lit both up with his own lighter and passed one to Darren. "Holy shit, man!"

"What-what dude? What's wrong?"

"Nothing's wrong. Everything is right. There's a joint in these smokes!"

"Save it, dude, actually better just to leave it there maybe. Shit, no man, don't spark it up." Doug displayed a big smile and lit the end of the joint with his cigarette.

"C'mon, one toke. What can happen?"

"Shit, didn't you hear what I said? Actually, didn't I hear what I said. Who gives a fuck? Pass it over." Darren took the joint and took a long pull on it as the drove off to their unholy destination where the beer could be had.

The effects of the pot were slight at first, it kind of snuck up on Darren. At first he began to think odd thoughts, then he felt the need to vocalize them.

"Dude, did you ever think about the universe like how it goes on forever?"

"Yeah, kind of, man. But that's outside, dude. All that isn't real. All that is real is right now, right here." Doug felt the sensation that the cab of the truck was his whole reality as he toked on the joint again.

"No man, this is the end. I mean, the universe... it ends you know, there has to be an end to everything don't you think?"

"The only end I can think of when I'm high is that blonde chick in my French class. She has the nicest end I've ever seen. I think if I ever got her to bed I would smoke her up and set up that strobe light I've got and just go to town man."

"Yeah, I get you there, dude. But think about it. Things can....

Suddenly a hard, loud SMASH!!! Stopped Darren in mid-sentence, sending the two boy's heads forward at an incredible rate into the dashboard, smacking them silly, or sillier than they were.

"Haaaah! Fuck man, I think I hit something." Indeed, a parked car had been the victim of Darren's mental wanderings. The two sat for a few minutes wondering what to do when Doug seemed to be the logical one for a change.

"Darren, man. This is a stolen truck! We NEED to get out of here."

"Haaaaahaaaaa.... okay, okay. I can do this." Darren said as he jammed the stick into reverse and backed up into a car parked behind him. After jamming it into forward he peeled off and they could hear the faint sound of RCMP sirens coming nearer.

Darren figured the best thing he could do would be to drive as fast as he could out of town, hopefully losing the cops but at his first turn, he saw distant lights flashing and coming towards him. He hit the brakes, then hit reverse and spun around backwards, letting off the gas just enough to push in the clutch and jam back into first at which time he took off like a rocket. Not three blocks later another

cruiser pulled out in front of him and stopped and so he instinctively turned onto the sidewalk and managed to evade the roadblock. For a while it looked safe, after he had taken another turn which would lead him into the Wetaskawin suburbs, where he had hoped he could park, turn out the lights and throw the pursuers off their trail, but a cop picked up his location somehow and roared up behind him. Hoping 4x4 meant he was unflippable, he took a fast corner a bit late and ended up sliding into a business in some strip mall.

Darren got out of the truck, about to wet himself at the amount of shit he was about to be in. The weird thing was that somehow Doug fed off of those surges of adrenalin and moments of intense stress. The Police Officer got out of his car with a shotgun drawn, loaded and pointing at the two. Needless to say he was a little less than happy at what Darren and Doug had put him and his friends through in the past little space of time. Doug for some reason decided he was bulletproof, or even buckshot proof and started to try and face down the Officer. He assumed what looked like a Karate pose he had learned from a video game and started making Ninja sounds. He moved in closer and the Cop didn't move, but said to him:

"Boy, you just better stay where you are or you're going to be in a world of hurt." This didn't phase Doug and he kept moving closer.

All of a sudden when he was about five feet away from the loaded gun, Doug yelled: "Run!!! Run now!!" And leapt forward, trying to grab ahold of the cop's shotgun. The cop would have had time to shoot both of them, but not with the interference Doug played.

"Boom!" Went the shotgun split seconds before Darren ran. If Darren had stayed, he might have been able to witness what would have been the most gruesome sight he would have ever seen, the actual amputation of a limb by a shotgun shot. Doug screamed in pain and although he was athletic and in good shape, Darren seemed to be able to double the speed of his sprint.

Darren didn't go back to his parent's place. He ran and kept running. When there was nothing left in him that could make him run further, he slowed to a walk, but kept moving. After a couple of days of eating berries and avoiding people, smearing animal shit on himself to throw off any dogs that might be hunting for him, he arrived in Edmonton. There he cleaned himself up, shoplifted some clothes, burned his ID and driver's license, then boarded a bus for the North Country, as far as he could go with money he had gotten selling things he had shoplifted. He bummed around for a while, working what under the table jobs he could, saying he was from the US and other bullshit.

Back in Wetaskawin, Doug was put on trial for all kinds of offences and the case dragged on. Somehow his parents, lacking in resources but not in love convinced him to go to a rehab centre and that lightened his sentence partially when it all came down. It didn't hurt either that the people there had to look at this young man who would be missing a limb for the rest of his life because of a mistake.

What didn't lighten the sentence was that even though it would have been the easiest thing in the world for him to do, all through the trial he insisted that everything was his idea, that Darren was pressured by him, Darren was a good kid, Darren was impressionable and younger than him. Warrants went out but Darren was never found. Doug got six years. When his time, minus good behaviour finally ended, he made the long walk out of the gates of the pen. He walked out, a free man and waiting at the gate was a black Mustang Fastback, he could tell right away it was a '67.

There was no one in it and though he had learned many tricks on the inside, he had no desire to steal it. The only thing was that there was a piece of card in the window that said "For you Doug" he pulled the sign off and got inside. There were keys in the ignition and there was a suitcase on the passenger seat. The car had been converted to automatic and had a special knob on the steering wheel so a person with one arm could drive it. Inside the suitcase was the registration for the car, a driver's license valid in Doug's name, an insurance card and likely around $50,000.00 in cash, and a CD.

Doug drove off and slid the CD into the car stereo and within a few seconds, Darren's voice came through the speakers. All that he said was, thanks man. If you ever want to get together for a game of quarters, take out a personal ad in the Calgary Herald, just say Doug needs a favour, then meet me the next day at The bar in the St.Regis, 12 noon. We've got a lot of catching up to do.

THE END

Leif Gregersen

THE CRAZY ONES

"You see Frank-o, I've been working for the city for twelve years, and the city takes care of me." The middle aged bus mechanic said to his coffee break companion.

"All I know about the city is they don't pay me enough to put up with the crap I have to put up with and whenever I see some guys working to improve roads that were built wrong in the first place, it's always the same: three guys staring a hole, waiting for quitting time and a cold beer."

"Well, what you have to understand is that when you are dealing with the city, your paycheque is one thing. It's one thing that you put in the bank, pay the mortgage, pay for the kid's school and sit tight. Then you look for opportunities."

"Opportunities. What you mean by that?"

"Well, in any job, Frankie, there are ways to pull in a little extra. Nothing serious, a little here, a little there. You see that scrap pile out back?" Andy pointed to a large yard with a pile of twisted metal, deposited without much rhyme or reason.

"Yeah, I see it. Kind of reminds me of my son's room."

"Well, in the twelve years I've been working here that pile has grown a little, shrunk a little. Sometimes a choice bit of metal leaves that yard and it isn't always to use as parts on a bus. Nothing huge, nothing serious. An axle here, a side panel or two there. It finds its way into the covered back of my truck and my truck finds its way to an out of town scrap metal business. Sometimes it pays enough for a few cases of beer and a carton of smokes, sometimes when times are really good I can take a little trip or, like now, I can pay for my kid's school fees. University isn't cheap."

"Doesn't anyone ever notice when stuff goes missing?" Frank asked.

"Frankie, my boy, I am not what you would call slow. Something comes out of that pile I make sure it can't be used for normal parts. Then, I get the forklift and move things around a bit so the pile looks the same. If the city were really on the ball I would never get away with it, but I am starting to believe that the city really doesn't care whether they get scrap prices, as long as they can keep the busses moving."

"So why you telling me all this?"

"Well, Frankie. I am telling you this because of opportunity. Today is your lucky day my friend. Today you are being offered a shot at something bigger than scrap metal. Something that could set you up for a good amount of time to come. You see, when you look for opportunities, you have to find the right people. I have been listening to and watching you. You live in an apartment. You have two kids. You need to move up but there's no money for a down payment on a house and renting is just like slavery. I just want you to think about what you might do to get enough to do just what you want to do. That's it. Just think about it and when you are sure you know how much you want this, get back to me."

"Well," Was all Frank could get out.

"No, no if's or but's. Just think for now and get back to me. Bring your family to my 2200 square foot house for a barbecue Sunday and we'll talk more. Okay?"

"Sure, see you then."

"Sunday it is."

| The Base Jumpers and Other Stories

////////////////////

That Sunday, Frank loaded his family into his 20 year-old two-tone four-door Chevrolet and drove halfway across the city of Edmonton into one of the fancier districts, and then found the street Frank lived on and followed it down, each house on the way seemingly more pretty and ideal than the last. These were the people who had houses where you didn't have to put two kids in one bedroom because some of the houses had at least 5 or 6 bedrooms. They had space for gardens in the back that wouldn't fill the yard but still provide fresh vegetables and such for most of the winter if stored properly.

These were not the homes of the ultra-rich, these were the homes of hard-working people that paid their mortgages on time year after year and were able near the end of their working days to trade up. There had to be some professional people here too, just starting their run up the housing ladder, but the former were more common.

These streets were made all the more beautiful by additions of front lawn flower gardens and 30 foot pine trees and elm trees lining the block on either side. It wasn't hard to spot Andy's house when they came near it. Out on the street was parked his rusty old Ford pickup with the covered box. As he pulled into the driveway, Frank noticed that Andy was fine-tuning his '76 Corvette. He had repainted it with a metallic shiny blue and red racing stripes. He had even had painted on flames over the rear wheel wells to add to the effect that this was a really fast car.

When Frank got out of his Chevy, he walked up to the Corvette in the garage and Andy wheeled himself out from under it, cigarette in his mouth and cold beer in one hand, crescent wrench in the other.

"Who wants to take a ride?" Andy yelled out to Frank's family. Both of his kids jumped up shouting and Chantelle, Frank's 9 year-old daughter got the first one.

As they pulled out of the driveway, Andy's wife came down to greet Frank. She had to be at least 40, but one could tell she took good care of herself and prided herself on her looks. Frank was almost surprised, he had expected to see a woman worn from years of raising kids and dealing with Andy's scoundrel-like ways. The first thing Frank said to her was,

"Hello, ma'am. Andy never told me he married a movie star." She smiled, and was clearly happy that yet another man found her attractive.

"You must be Frank. I'm Amanda. Did your children bring their bathing suits?" A pool was an extreme luxury in Edmonton, with the short summer and all.

"Oh, we didn't even think to bring them. Or towels. Honey, is there anyway you can go get the kids' suits while Andy and I fire up the barbecue?"

"Oh no, don't worry about that. Hi, sorry I didn't introduce myself." Amanda shot a glance at Frank as though the two shared a secret. Then she smiled and said, "I'm Amanda, and we have lots of suits, washed and everything. Plenty of towels, too."

"Daddy, I want to ride in the car!" Frank's seven year-old said.

"You'll get your chance Danny. Have to wait until they come back."

"I'm Helen." Frank's wife said, seeming a bit suspicious of everything going on. "Do you and Andy have any kids?"

"Three. All in University, none of them with a job.One's in Psychology and the other two computers. I like to say in a way they are all trying to grab a brain. You and Frank just have the two? They're adorable."

"We love 'em." Frank said.

"Our girl wants to be an actress, our boy wants to be a pilot. We would settle for a play writer and a..."

Suddenly the blue and red Corvette appeared, Andy driving, cigarette in his mouth still-or maybe it was another one. Regardless, Frank's daughter got out, left the door open for Danny and hopped up and down, giddy as a tittering schoolgirl. Danny jumped in and Amanda shouted towards the car,

"When you get back bring little Danny out back, and find him a swimsuit!" Andy waved his hand and peeled out, filling the young boy with glee. "Okay, let's go get ready to have some fun. What's your name girl?"

"Chantelle." The young one said as she smiled through braces.

"I think you might fit a nice one-piece I have. Bit too small for me but should fit you okay. Come on you two, no need to worry about Andy, if it's one thing he knows how to do, it's drive his car." The group walked up the driveway and into the house.

Out in back of the house where most people would put their vegetable garden, there was a kidney-bean shaped pool with a one metre diving board. Amanda took Chantelle in to get a bathing suit and Frank and Helen went and sat down near the pool on a wooden bench.

"So tell me again how this guy is going to help us get a house?"

"Not so loud. I wasn't supposed to tell anyone. He just said he could help and I was supposed to think about things, you know, prioritize, and then come over here and see him." Frank replied.

"Well, all I can think is that these people didn't get this place and that car honestly. He makes no more than you for heaven's sake."

"That's what I was trying to tell you. He makes the same but he keeps his eyes open, opportunity knocks now and then and he takes advantage. How do you know he doesn't have a side business or his wife inherited some money. There could be lots of reasons. I thought about things like he said and I think there are a lot of things that I would do if it meant getting a decent place to live for our kids. Do you know that when I came home the other day there was a drunk sleeping in the elevator? He had even pissed himself."

"I know. It's awful, but all we can do is our best. I never had the benefit of a parent who could spend time with me. What if this thing makes you go out of town and spend a lot of late nights working. That won't make our kids love us any more. They may grow up to resent things we've done. I don't want that to happen."

"Let's just see what Andy has to say. Then we can go back to our hovel." He replied with a deep note of sarcasm.

///////////////////////////////

The next few hours went by fairly smoothly. Frank grew more and more anxious to get to talk with Andy, but Andy remained the life of the party, showing Danny how to play pool, roasting up hamburgers and their buns after putting butter on them. The selection of beef was superb and with the buns toasted they seemed to be the best beef burgers Frank and his family ever had. After their meal Chantelle and Danny wanted to jump right back in the pool but their Mom would have none of it. She didn't want them to get cramps in the pool so Amanda suggested they go take a nap while the men played pool and the women got to know each other. Everyone was happy with that but Helen, but she had her eye on the last burger and she knew Amanda wouldn't take it, so in a way everyone was okay with that plan.

Andy and Frank went downstairs to the pool room and Andy closed the door and locked it behind them and then Andy took a cue and randomly clicked the balls together.

"Frank, you're a man like me, right?"

"In what sense?"

"You love your family. You love kids, they mean the world to you."

"Of course, but I think the similarities end there."

"I guess you're wondering how I can afford all this. The pool, the rec room, the big house."

"Seems like a little more than scrap metal income." Frank said judgmentally.

"It is. And you might have been wondering about Amanda."

"Just a little. I was a bit curious how a woman with her figure could have had three kids of University age."

"Frankie, you're not a stupid man. I'm going to be straight with you. I love my kids but I sometimes think I never loved my first wife. For a while everything was great, we had a good life together, I had a great job, little extra money working on cars at home. But it wore me out. After a while I decided I wasn't the kind of person who could work every god damned day of my life, support three kids and a wife by 12 hours of dirty filthy labor and go nowhere, accomplish nothing."

"I feel the same way. No way to get ahead. Sometimes it makes me want to kill myself, but then I look at my kids and I know that's not an option." Frank replied.

"Well, I'm just going to lay it out for you. This house isn't mine. It's Amanda's. She bought most of it from what she stuck her last husband for, and I lined up to be number two. I have a good life, but things are falling apart. Of course the kids are mine and my ex-wife's, but with alimony and school fees I'm going to end up where you are, stuck in an apartment only I'll be there by myself and I will have to tell my kids after riding the gravy train they will no longer be able to attend school and get the shot at a decent life I never had." Andy told him, a wave of sadness going over him.

"Well, what can be done? I'm no criminal." Frank answered.

"I've thought of something. Something pretty serious, it's fraud but so are a lot of things. I have a life insurance policy, $500,000. Here's how the plan goes: I'm going to work on a bus, fix the brakes wrong, I can make it look like a mistake anyone could make. Then I need to test drive it but I'll get you to do that, with me in the back. We drive it up a steep hill like Grierson Road and then turn it around, jump out at the top of the hill, let the bus go off the road with an incendiary timer on the gas tank, the bus goes down, everything is burned, I hide out, leave town, my kids get the money, and I pay you $50,000 out of the money I have stashed from all these years in the scrap business just to say I never got off the bus."

"That all sounds well and good, but it doesn't seem to do much for your end."

"Well, I avoid a messy divorce, buy a US passport, with a new name and head to Florida, free of the burden of alimony and knowing I did what I could for my kids."

"Can I have more time to think about this?"

"Not much. I have a schedule. First you need to swear secrecy, then later this week it all goes down." Andy said, looking quite serious.

"Swear on my mother's grave."

"Can't even tell your wife."

"Done."

"So do you have a verdict for me now?"

Frank thought about all the times he had been kicked in the teeth. When he was 18 and a shoo-in for a football scholarship and had an excruciatingly painful broken femur that made his scholarship impossible. Then he thought about school exams where he had slept in for one final and missed an honors average and entrance to the program he wanted by 1.2%. All these times he had worked hard and tried to do the right thing and now couldn't even house his family properly. "I'm in." He said, and shook Andy's hand.

/////////////////////

    Andy had planned out things so that everything would go off late Wednesday night. The first thing he did was invite Frank to hang around that night in front of others just so all the bases would be covered. His aptitude with mechanics served him well because he was able to make a flammable explosive that would be set off with a timer. On Monday he had worked on a bus and put thin brake pads on it so it would squeal and a random driver would take it in for repair. That was the bus he would use. His plan called for him to make it look like the brakes had failed by accident and caused the vehicle to veer off the road, with sparks setting the gas tank on fire. It called for precise timing, he had driven the route at night a number of times at differing speeds just to be able to set the incendiary timer perfectly, but with a few seconds of extra time.

Wednesday evening came and Frank was near to being a wreck with nerves. Having everything ready, Andy convinced him to have two beers, no more to calm him down but not enough to fail a breathalyzer. The time for them to go came closer and Andy took a walk through the bus, looking for anything he may have forgotten.

Andy had figured the perfect time to leave would be 9:00. Not many people on the road, the late summer sun gone down, they would be fairly free to get out and push the bus down the hill if they had to. He was glad he had given himself extra time though because he had realized that the odd movie goer may be on the road but that didn't mean too much. At least it wasn't discount Tuesday.

"Are you ready, Frank?" Andy asked.

"If we have to wait until I'm ready we'll be here all week."

"Can you handle this? We can call it off you know." Andy replied, sounding more human than he had seemed in the past while.

"No, I want this. I want it just as much as you do." Frank said.

"Then let's do it."

With that, Frank got into his seat, adjusted the mirror and started up the engine, then adjusted the seat and pulled out of the bus barns. Andy even had their route planned, 118 avenue to Wayne Gretzky Drive (this was Edmonton), then down to the River Valley, across to Grierson Hill, turn around and go down the hill (with the alibi of testing the brakes) and then jump out as the bus is still rolling, Andy takes off and Frank calls the switchboard, and everyone goes home wealthy.

There was just one problem.

Just as the bus with Andy and Frank on it came to the bridge before Grierson Hill, a sight that all too many people get to see appeared in front of them. Some teenager in a Pontiac had flown at top speed across the bridge and ran right into the back end of a small economy car driven by two people in their 20's with a baby in the back of the car. Instinct made Frank stop and instinct made them get out and help. Andy raced back to the gas tank to stop the timer on his incendiary device and once done, he went first to the teenager's car and was very nearly sick at the sight of him. The boy had a seatbelt on but it didn't stop him from smashing his face into the steering wheel. He felt for a ceratoid pulse, but there was none. He had bled to death before they had even got there, so Andy went to do what he could to help Frank.

"Take our baby!" The woman screamed. "Get him to the hospital!" It was hard to tell who was screaming louder, the mother or the child. Frank took charge.

"Will do, just stop for a second, we can all go." Frank said trying to sound calm.

"Please, we're fine. Our baby is hurt, help him first!" The man said.

"Okay, get in the bus, we'll do everything we can!" Andy declared loudly.

The two got on the bus and Frank jumped into the driver's seat and floored the gas pedal to get up the hill as quick as he could. The woman began to calm down, Andy often had that soothing effect on people. He had taken Industrial First Aid through work and had carefully checked the baby for injuries and reassured the mother that there wasn't any, he just needed to cry it out and he would be okay.

As the bus neared the top of the ridge, without driver input the brakes seized on the right hand side. At first Frank thought he could handle it which he may have but he was half involved in the state of his passengers. The front part of the bus smashed through the barricade running all the way up the road but as this was happening, Frank slammed on the brakes and a third of the bus was off the edge.

"Frank! Get the hell back here, we need your weight!" Andy screamed. Frank came back without hesitation.

The two young parents didn't know what to do, they were paralyzed with fear. Andy and Frank managed to get the left side emergency exit open and after some convincing, got the baby's mother and father off the bus.

"You next, Frank!" Andy demanded.

"Me? What about the kid?"

"I'll take care of the kid. You can't pass it to those two. They're out of their minds with fear. You get out, I'll pass you the kid and everything will be okay. Everything will be called off."

"I'm only doing this because I think you're an asshole, you know."

Andy seemed to betray the fear on his face that didn't appear on Frank's. "You're a hero, Frank." He said.

"Yeah, that's right, and I'm going to save you too." He replied.

"I'm just a broken down old cheat. I was never going to pay you your cut."

"That's okay. I told my wife and she was going to turn you in."

"Honor among thieves. Get the hell out of here." Frank squeezed himself through the exit, then Andy gently passed the baby out, then he stood up and walked up to the front of the bus, causing it to tilt even more. He gave

Frank a crisp salute as the massive vehicle tumbled down into the River Valley, catching fire at the bottom.

/////////////////////////

As things settled, the baby Andy had saved turned out to be fine. There were two losses to mourn, Andy and the teenage driver. Frank didn't really know how to feel about it, in some ways Andy wasn't really a friend, he was just a partner in crime. Later when his will was being settled, Frank learned that Andy had indeed left him $50,000.00. At the funeral he got to meet Andy's kids. They seemed nice enough, but on the whole spoiled. They were all thinking they would have to get jobs or sell Andy's only possession, his Corvette but the Insurance money was a surprise. He even had the lawyer say to them they weren't told about the Insurance because he wasn't stupid enough to give someone a reason for him to die, family or not. The city gave Frank a citation and Andy a medal, which he was buried with, along with his only two real friends, as his will stated, a pack of cigarettes and a six-pack. One thing was for sure, Frank would never forget him or stop wondering if they would meet one day in heaven and he could thank him for the down payment on the house he eventually bought.

THE END

STINGRAY GRADUATION

It was a sunny spring day in the city of Edmonton. Here, sunlight came at a premium. They only get it 5 or 6 months of the year and they pay for it with an equal amount of rain and snow, but mostly snow.

Carmine sat in the trailer he used for an office at his car lot. He had done good this week, he had gotten two cars at auction for $225 and $265 and had sold them for a profit of around $2,000.00. Normally he didn't rip of friends like he did with these two cars, but he had something big he had been working on. Something that made his phone ring just as he was considering a trip to the Italian Supermarket for a sandwich and some orange pop which he might put a little vodka in later.

"Hello. Who's this?" Carmine answered the phone in a nasal and brash manner.

"This is Gianni. We got your car ready for you." Came the reply.

"I'll be there in forty-five seconds." Carmine joked. At least half-joked, Gianni's Garage was just across the street from Carmine's lot. Nothing was too far from anything in Little Italy. You could go into some of the bars around there and get anything-a pound of coke, the company of a young woman. Even a fancy car. But for the most part Carmine had put those things behind him. He had a reason to.

Carmine left his car and went over to Gianni's Garage and when he went out with Gianni to open the door to his beautiful car he was awestruck to say the very least. Here was an orange Corvette, with yellow flames on the sides all decked out and perfectly restored. He had sent the car in for the full restoration and the last thing it was getting now was an engine. He wanted his son to have nothing but the very best.

"This is sweet my friend, very sweet. Start it up." He said almost judgementally.

"This things purrs like a kitten. Just listen." The mechanic started up the Stingray and the sound of it lived up to what he said. The engine sounded perfect, perfectly in tune and perfectly powerful. Carmine's son was not going to know what hit him when he learned what his high school graduation present was going to be.

"Now what do I owe you?"

"A steal. A pittance. Four large."

"Four! I thought you said you could do it for 2" Carmine blurted out.

"Yeah. Install it and rebuild the engine for two, but I had to get another engine. That last 350 was so screwed up there was no point in a rebuild."

"Why didn't you call me about this. Fuck! You know what I had to do to get the cash?"

"Yeah, yeah. I know, sell cars, sell this, sell that. You better sell something else in a hurry because if you don't come up with the cash I won't feel bad at all about selling this car to someone ele and keeping my tradesmen's lien and giving you the change. I've put up with your bullshit for 10 years now and I never seem to win."

"Alright, alright." Carmine quacked. "Hold onto the registration. I'll get the cash in a couple of hours."

"I want your license, too, and that gold ring you always wear."

"What the fuck! You think I'm some kind of bank machine?"

"No, I just know you. Give me the ring. It's the one thing I know you'll come back for."

"Okay, okay. You know if I didn't love my son like I do I would likely punch you in the nose."

"How can you say that? We're like family!"

Carmine let out a huff and got in the corvette and gave a little too much gas and heard his wheels spin. This car had some balls he thought to himself, and let it open a little heading down 97 street to Tony's bar. When he got there all the old Italians were sitting outside at tables in the sun smoking and telling each other the same stories they had been telling for years. Seeing a flashy Stingray pull into the parking lot caught their attention.

"Hey, Carmine!" One of the younger ones yelled. "Where'd you steal that?" Carmine answered as he usually did to smart assed remarks, with his middle finger. He got out of the car and felt the hot gaze of a streetwalker standing in front of the pub which made him try and conceal his beer gut by folding his jacket over it. When he got in the door he looked at his watch-it was just after 12. His son got out of school at 3:00pm, that should just give him enough time. The Graduation Ceremony wouldn't start until 6:00. Out of here by 2:00, ready by 3:00, time to let him take the car out with his girlfriend and think about what a great dad he was-or had become in the recent past.

The object of Carmine Dipini's mission to this place was the six machines up against the wall. He just couldn't face the idea of not giving his son the car with full title, so he figured he could break the bank here which was the only way he knew how to get the money... aside from doing a favour for one of the tough looking men who were always there, always at the same table. He didn't want to think about going into business with them. He knew it would be practically getting into bed with them.

Carmine sat at the bar and drank a few beers, then his friend Tony, who owned the bar came up and brought him a bourbon to loosen him up. He knew the man would get a little shaky around this time of day if he didn't have a little liquid courage of the 40% variety to get him centered.

"Tell me your troubles, friend." Tony said in a reassuring manor.

"Gotta raise two large in 2 hours."

"Got anything to do with that flashy car you got out there?"

"It's a gift for my boy. He's graduating high school today."

"Little Joey! Hey, this calls for a celebration! On me." Tony poured out two more shots and one for himself, then the two men drank and shared stories about what Carmine's son was like as a baby. Then one of the gambling machines opened up and Carmine excused himself and took a fresh beer over to it.

He played for a while and it seemed like the machine had gone cold for him. Then out of nowhere he hit a jackpot and was up about $700 from what he started with-not enough. He decided to keep trying but needed more beers to take the edge off. He liked gambling like this. He even seemed to like it when he lost because it excited him. He would do anything to be able to gamble all the time, play poker, go to the casino and play the slots. He kept the odds long and thus had to usually wait a long time to hit in the hundreds, but you never knew. There had been times he put in his last $5 and walked away with grocery money for a week. But there had been a lot of times when he put in hundreds and went home half drunk and hungry, not even having enough money for gas. This time he knew: this time he was sure. Why play if you aren't sure? This had to be God's way of rewarding the pure of heart he sometimes thought. Then when he lost he blamed the devil.

Up and down he went, all over the place, numbing the fear and the excitement with more booze. Then, seemingly after no time had passed it was all gone-every cent. The $2,000.00 he was going to pay for the car-not counting the $700 he had been up or the $2,000 he had needed to make. All of it was gone. He stopped for a minute, leaned his head into his hand and it slowly dawned on him that he was truly fucked. No more chances, no car, no present. How could a loving God do this to a 17 year-old kid he thought to himself. He went back to the bar, and Tony brought him a beer. He looked at his watch. 4:17. He had been gambling all that time.

"Tony." He said with no emotion in his voice.

"Yes my friend?"

"You like the Oilers?"

"Me? No, I always like the Bruins. Boston is my team. At least in hockey."

"The Bruins then. You like the Bruins."

"Yes, I just said so."

"Well, I think the Oilers will win. What do you think about that?"

"You want to bet me?"

"That's what I'm getting at."

"The game's almost over. The Oilers are behind."

"I'm willing to bet you $4,000.00 the Oilers win and if I lose you can have my car."

"I'll take that bet!" Came a voice from behind them. They didn't need to look. It came from Lenny's table. Lenny the gangster.

"I lose, the car is yours."

"A fair bet. Now we have just 17 minutes to wait for me to drive it."

The whole room seemed to stop and look at the two of them, fixate on the TV screen. The score was Boston 2, Edmonton 0. If He tried to get out of it or if there was any monkey business, he would never survive to see his son go on to College. He would either have to go far away or pay the piper. And the piper didn't take credit notes.

Carmine sat for the next 17 minutes, drinking a beer then drinking a shot. At least he had a tab left but if things didn't go well he had no way to pay it. His car lot would go to Lenny when he lost. But he had a chance, albeit a small one.

Carmine heard every word the announcers said, heard every cheer, but never bothered to look up at the screen. Time ticked by, a goal was scored, then another. Someone came up to him and told him the Oilers now had a chance. A chance. All his life on a chance.

Then the game went into overtime. There was a penalty and the Oilers lost a man. It was power-play time for the Bruins and in a last ditch effort the Oilers pulled their Goalie. Every person in the room was riveted to the TV screen. Suddenly the bar erupted in cheers of victory and happiness and Carmine took his last shot, then put it down upside down on the table. He walked over to Lenny and asked him what just happened.

"Your boys won, Carmine. You did good. You're lucky I pay my debts." The aging Mafioso reached down into his sock and came up with an ankle wallet packed with hundred dollar bills. He counted out forty of them and handed them over. He wobbled a little but Carmine walked to the car with the money and gently drove down the street to pay Gianni. The car was his. Now it would be his son's. Now all the crap and the garbage, the cheating on his mother and the divorce could all be washed away, now in one stroke he would make up for all the birthdays he missed, all the soccer games, all the Christmasses. And maybe as they shared a love of cars they could spend some time together, really get to know each other. He looked forward to the idea of showing his boy how to change oil, how to set the timing on an engine, how to get the most power out of a car as one puts it through the gears.

The car felt good, it felt fit and lean and efficient. It cornered like a dream, and when he drove it into the parking lot of the apartment building where Joey and his Mother lived, he stepped on the gas a little. Maybe it was the booze, maybe it was because he went too fast. Maybe he was getting old and couldn't see so well. The boy was wearing a dark suit for his Grad. He ran into something, heard a clunk and a sort of 'smash' as it whiplashed into the front window cracking it, then rolled over the top of the beautiful car. He knew he hit something he just didn't know what. When he got out he saw it. Carmine had run into his son and his son lay on the pavement, his head crushed, the life bleeding out of him.

Two months later Carmine pleaded guilty to drunk driving causing death and was given ten years in prison as a sentence. He had the last laugh on the judge because he never spent his ten years in prison. Two months after he went to the penitentiary he hung himself with a sheet.

THE END

WOULDN'T IT BE NICE

"Babies. I want to have lots of babies. Big fat ones that look like both of us and my crazy Uncle Ron." Jason said to Amy who broke out in giggles.

"Jason!" She scolded. "We're only 18. Do you have any idea how much we'll have to go through and how many people you will meet in University before we are old enough to handle babies!"

"Yeah, I know, and I don't care. You're my girl, now and forever," Jason said and kissed his true love's cute, rounded cheek. In response, she ran her hand over her favorite part of him, his bumpy and muscled stomach and up his chest under his shirt. "Man, you really know how to drive me crazy woman!" Jason said and moved in for a kiss but was interrupted by his Dad flinging open the door to the den they were in.

"Jason, I think it's time for Amy to go home." It seemed every time he started to have a little fun he was interrupted, but he knew he would soon have the rest of his life with Amy. He told his Dad okay and Amy got up and he got to admire her curvy backside as she walked towards the door that had just been flung open.

"How does that Beach Boys song go? Wouldn't it be nice if we were older, we could say goodnight and still be together..."

"Soon enough, lover," Amy teased, her brown and alluring eyes and long curly dark brown hair making him want to follow her to her car and hope they could have a chance to get somewhere before she had to be home. He almost got up in hopes of trying, but he looked at his watch and it was 10:30pm, already past the time she had to be home. He would have to wait for an opportune time, which could be a week or two since he had a volleyball tournament that weekend and would be out of town.

"Goodnight, Babe," Jason said and got up to kiss her goodnight. "Dream about me." She smiled and said:

"You know it, gorgeous." That word: gorgeous, made him quiver all over. No other girl he had gone out with had called him that. She walked down the hall and out to her car and he spent a fitful night wishing they could have at least necked for a while before she left.

The weekend came around and Amy saw Jason off on the school bus to his volleyball tournament and kissed him right in front of all his teammates as the bus was loading. A few of his buddies hung their heads out the window and cheered them on and then he reluctantly boarded the vehicle and soon was headed off out of town.

That night Amy got a call from a friend and with it an invitation to crash a house party that some of the basketball team would be going to. In the back of her mind she wondered if Brent would be there. Brent was her former boyfriend from her days in grade ten and she didn't know what would happen if they ran into each other. Part of her wondered what he thought of her after all this time. It had been two years since he had dumped her. When she got to the party later that night, sure enough, there he was, and he wasn't with anyone. As she sucked back a few beers and the odd shot that was offered her she had looked over at him a number of times not knowing what he was thinking. Finally he seemed to look back and she was feeling a little tipsy so she walked over to talk with him.

Amy and Brent talked for a while. She found out he had won a scholarship to an out of province school. The party got noisy so after trying to shout at each other for a while they decided to go up to a bedroom and chat. She was really surprised how much Brent had matured and they talked for a long time about their going out and Brent apologized for dumping her, explaining that he had always had a hard time with commitments and it was actually his friends that had convinced him to do it.

After sitting in the bedroom for an hour, Amy got hot and took her jacket off and Brent started to massage her shoulders. As he was doing this she talked for a while in a beer-buzz kind of way about how she wanted to marry Jason as soon as they were done school and how it felt so good that she could finally talk to Brent about their relationship. But just then the door flew open.

"Amy! What the fuck!" Jason yelled at her.

"Jason! This is Brent, we were just talking about you!"

"I'm sure you were!" He yelled and ran over and grabbed Brent and started hitting him.

"Jason! It's not what you think!" Brent yelled while trying to dodge a flurry of fists. "We used to go out-we were just talking, man!" Finally Brent got sick of being a punching bag and grabbed Jason and threw him roughly to the floor. Then he held him down with his foot and opened the door to the bedroom and called out to his buddies. Three or four incredibly fit basketball players came running upstairs to his aid and started to lay a beating on Jason.

"Stop! Stop! You can't do this to him! He's my boyfriend!" Suddenly the guy whose house it was came in.

"What's going on here? All of you, out!" Amy helped Jason to his feet and the scuffle continued when they got out of the front door. Amy pushed Brent's buddies away from them and then her and Jason got into Jason's car. The basketball players were pounding on his windows as he pulled away and Amy took out a handkerchief and dabbed at the bloody spots on Jason's face.

"What the fuck were you doing in there with him!" Jason said, nearly in tears.

"Nothing! He's my ex. We were just talking. He's leaving town. I just wanted to get some closure, remember the guy I told you about that dumped me in grade ten?"

"Don't you understand..." Just then, as if out of nowhere all of the world stopped suddenly. The next second was like a thousand years and a thousandth of a second all at once. Jason had not been paying attention, he was dizzy from his blows, weak from playing volleyball

all evening and distracted by Amy. Jason's car smashed head-on into another coming from the opposite direction and all Jason could remember for the next while was that split second of twisting metal and shattering glass. He was injured badly and didn't wake up until four days later in the hospital. He woke up and he could feel his feet and his hands and could move them but at first it was very difficult for him to understand what had happened. He tried to call out for someone but his mouth was dry as a bone. With all the strength he could muster, he reached for a carafe of water that had been set on a tray by his bed and it slipped off when he reached for it. By a stroke of luck a nurse had heard it and came to talk to him.

"Mr. East." The nurse said to him, picking up the mess and wiping the water up with a towel. "It's good to see you stirring. Your parents just went home a little while ago. Things were touch and go for you for a while."

"Uuuhhhfff... Uffff... wh...at happened?" Jason asked her through parched lips.

"You were in a car accident, remember?"

"Ju...st... just a little..." He replied. "Where is Amy...?"

"Your girlfriend didn't make it, Jason. I'm sorry to be the one to have to tell you."

"She... she... what?"

"Your girlfriend died in the accident." She said, and with that Jason passed out again.

The next day Jason woke up and he could remember the words the nurse had spoken the day before, he could just barely believe them. His parents came and brought him some chocolate and a book of puzzles. They said very little, just stared at him mostly and he just stared back. Jason had a dead expression on his face.

It didn't take Jason too long to heal up. He had a couple of broken ribs and a lot of bruising but soon with some Physiotherapy and time to heal he was doing physically better. Spiritually and emotionally though, he wasn't doing all that well. After a few weeks he was sent home and for the next two months he did very little other than watch TV and ask his Mom to get him things. He would lay and sleep for a dozen hours and eat very little. His parents were soon at the end of their wits, their boy had been so strong and dynamic before all this had happened.

At the end of the two months, Jason's Dad came to him and offered to take him on a cruise. It was the only thing he could think of that could possibly get him out of his funk. What he didn't know was that the cruise he offered was one that Jason had been saving for to take Amy on. His father was dumbfounded when the supposedly good news was met with more apparent sadness and some tears.

His parents left that night to attend a conference and Jason finally got the nerve up. He took every pill from Tylenol to sleeping pills that had been left in the cupboard in the bathroom over the years. He went back to bed and laid down, hoping this would be the end to his pain. His parents came home that night and his Dad went to check on him and he seemed to be soundly sleeping but when he listened for the snoring sound his son usually made, he only heard a shallow breath. He didn't think much of it but when he went to get his toothbrush, Jason's Dad noticed right away that there were a lot of pills missing. He called 911 and paramedics rushed over to save his boy's life.

Once again Jason woke up in the hospital, but this time it was a Psychiatric Hospital. He didn't realize at first if he was alive or not but when he wandered out in the hallway and saw the polished tile floors and other patients in pajamas he figured out what had happened. The first thing he did was go to the nurses' desk and ask what was going on.

"Hello, Jason, I'm Tracy. I'm your nurse today." A young woman told him from behind the desk. "How are you feeling?"

"I'm feeling like I should have taken enough pills." Jason said. His head was pounding and his whole body wanted to go back to sleep.

"You shouldn't talk like that!" Tracy replied. "A lot of people are very worried about you."

"Not my girlfriend's parents!" Jason declared and walked off back to where he had slept. To his surprise, Tracy followed him.

"Jason, we know what happened with your girlfriend. You have to understand that it was an accident.

Things like that happen every day. I'm sure even if they don't know now your girlfriend's parents will come to forgive you. From what I understand you weren't drinking or using drugs and you weren't texting. That means you either made a mistake or someone else did." It really surprised Jason that this lady knew all of this, but still he didn't say anything back to her though for the first time since the fateful night Amy died he felt somewhat good.

The next few days were kind of strange. He found out soon enough that he wasn't allowed off the Psychiatric Ward he was on and he wasn't allowed regular clothes or a jacket. He had been told that after he got in to see the Doctor he would be assessed and then he could have more privileges. Jason didn't really care much, either way. One night though, he was sleeping and he heard a loud wailing coming from the next room. It went on for quite a while and it was loud and extremely disturbing so he went to see what was going on. Nothing could have prepared him in his life for what he was about to see. It was a young man (apparently) who had been burned beyond imagination over most of his body. He must have been brought in while Jason was asleep, and it looked like he was in some serious pain.

"Hey dude what's the problem?" Jason asked him.

"I need some water." Came the grumble.

"I can do that for you, but why can't the nurses?"

"I don't know. Maybe they are lazy." Jason went and got the water and came back and held up the guy's head and poured a little in his mouth. He didn't understand why, but for some reason he felt drawn to this poor person.

"Hey, dude. What's your name?"

"Chris." He said

"Hey Chris. I'm Jason."

"I have a brother named Jason."

"Really? What's he do for a living?"

"He died in the fire." Chris said 'the fire' as though there only ever was one, and Jason understood. Half of this guy's face was skin grafts and most of one of his arms. It looked painful.

"Are you in pain?"

"All the time."

From there, Jason and Chris began to be friends. Jason made a couple of more trips for water and even helped him into his wheelchair when it was time to go to the bathroom. Each day after that, the two were nearly inseparable, Jason would wheel him where he wanted to go and they would eat together and talk for hours. Then one day Chris asked him why he was there, it was a subject that most people in Psychiatric wards try to avoid, but here it was staring in his face. Jason looked down and started to tell the story of how he had this wonderful girlfriend and then one day he thought she was cheating on him and found her with an ex-boyfriend at a party and then said how he accidentally killed her in a car accident and then later tried to kill himself.

"What!" Chris exclaimed. "Your girlfriend died in a car accident and you thought that was good enough reason to die?"

"Yeah, what's wrong with that?" Jason said, thinking that Chris should have understood.

"Look at me! Look at my face! Look at my arm! Do you think I'll ever have a girlfriend?"

"I don't know. Maybe. It depends more on personality." Jason answered.

"You've got everything. You've got your health. You've got your looks. Do you think this Amy person would want you moping around and then killing yourself because of an accident?"

"But your fire was an accident. Why is it different?"

"My fire wasn't an accident!! I started it for fun. I was playing with matches and my brother died! God will never forgive me! Even if you were in the wrong, all you have to do is unburden your sins and God will forgive you. Me-look at me. I'll never play sports. I'll never have a job. I'll never have anything!!!" A frightening look of anger crossed Chris' face as he said these things. In that moment, Jason saw that there was an ugliness to self-pity and anger and it had little to do with scars. Jason got up and stopped going to see Chris, stopped talking to him.

The next day it was finally time for Jason to see his doctor and it didn't seem like much. Jason tried to explain that he tried to kill himself out of guilt and didn't think he would ever come to terms with it. The Doctor didn't seem to take long to decide on a course of action.

"Jason, after talking with your parents about your childhood and a few other things, and getting feedback from the nursing staff, I have come to the conclusion that you are prone to depression. And it is a dangerous form of depression, severe enough for you to try and kill yourself. The way you attempted suicide was unusual, mostly we see people trying it to get attention but you really wanted to die. We are going to try you out on a course of Electro Convulsive Therapy and then see what we can do to stabilize you with medications." Jason's face dropped. He had seen what ECT was like in movies and they seemed pretty scary. As he talked with the Doctor, some of his fears were allayed but not all of them. What wasn't an option was whether or not to have the treatments, the doctor's mind was made up.

For the next month Jason went through two treatments a week and for a while his memory was fairly scrambled. He actually caught himself having a good time here and there until he remembered that he was supposed to be in grief and mourning. When the treatments stopped he was put on an anti-depressant and started going to support groups. All this while he had seen Chris around but didn't talk to him. Finally one day he started to realize how stupid it had been and how right Chris was in chastising him. He went in to see Chris and they talked for a long time. Chris was still a bit bitter but seemed to be more at peace with himself. They went back to being friends, one day Jason decided to try and cheer

Chris up and brought in a balloon and for an hour the two of them batted the ball around, playing a game like volleyball and for the first time Jason thought he heard it from him, Jason laughed and giggled at the fun they were having.

"Jason, there is something I need to tell you."

"What's that?"

"This place isn't a Mental Hospital."

"Okay, whatever. What is it then?"

"Are you Catholic?"

"I was baptised Catholic and went to church a few times."

"I hate to be the one to say it. You didn't survive that accident." Jason felt very creeped out, and his first thought was that Chris was insane. It didn't scare him though, in the time he had been in that place he had met a lot of insane people. He had no clue that Chris was that bad. Then he looked down at his feet for some reason and right in front of his eyes his leg and foot muscles began to wither. As he was looking down, he saw a drop of blood land on the floor and touched his head which seemed to have been bashed in.

"So what is this place then?" Jason said, filling with fear.

"Purgatory."

"Purgatory?"

"You remember, where you go to work off your sins. Where you are tested to see if you go on to Heaven or Hell."

"So where am I going?" As he asked this, the body image right in front of him of Chris' burned form changed to a spiritual one, like a ghost and a pair of wings unfolded from behind his back.

"You're coming with me to Heaven. At first we didn't know if you would make it. You were spiteful, jealous, angry, bitter, you hated yourself and tried to kill yourself and leave your family in all that pain. But what you did here, to a poor burned up kid, gave him his last joy while asking for nothing in return, that sealed the deal. You can come with me now." Chris stood up in his Angel form and put his arms around Jason and started to beat his wings. In moments they flew up through the ceiling of the hospital and up into the sky. They ended up far up in space, they didn't have bodies anymore that needed breath or atmosphere and Jason's personal Angel hurled him off towards a great white light far off in space. As he travelled towards it, he could hear Amy, along with a choir of angels singing. She was singing with the voice of an Opera star, and a symphony orchestra was backing up the vocals. It was hard to make out the words at first, but as he drew nearer he knew it was her and she was singing, "Wouldn't it be nice if we were older…."

THE END

Leif Gregersen

THE RED WOLF

Carl Larsen sat at his desk, killing time, trying to get enough work done to satisfy his boss but not enough to stand out, just as he had done in various desks for the past 30 years. 30 years! Where had the time gone. What had happened to the adventuresome, athletic youth who dreamed of competing in Olympic skiing competitions? The bold athlete who chased down everything with a skirt until he felt the reward of conquest completed in the inner circles of his friends and in his bed.

Thinking of these memories never made him feel better or work harder. There was only a half hour left in the day, actually in the week, it was Friday. What had Friday meant to him when he was younger? Parties, drinking, sex, camaraderie, the whole nine yards. Now? Now the weekend just meant two days alone watching television and sleeping in until the Sunday paper came. It stank.

Well, to hell with squeezing in another half an hour of work he didn't care about, to hell with it. Carl manoeuvred his computer mouse to a new section and found a mindless video game he had played once or twice before when he first had to learn about these damn new machines. He happily clicked away, oblivious to the fact that his supervisor was in clear view of his computer screen the whole time.

Carl was about to snicker to himself at how the simple game could help pass the time when he felt a hand touch his shoulder and he nearly jumped out of his skin.

"Mr. Larsen!" Came the harsh sounding words along with the intrusive hand. "Is there any reason why you are using company time to play some childish game? I thought you knew better than that."

Carl was embarrassed, but he stood his ground. "Same reason you take two hours for lunch when Mr. Melnyk isn't here, Rich. I can't stand this place."

"Mr. Larsen, I am beginning to think that your attitude is getting worse and worse. Why didn't you take your early retirement when you had the chance. You say you don't like it here. Come on, be honest with me. We've known each other since this company was located in a boiler room."

"I can't expect you to understand, Rich. I lost Lucy three years ago and nothing has been the same." Carl replied. "If I had to stick around my apartment all day every day waiting for a pension cheque to come once a month I would lose it."

"You know, Carl. I think I know what you need. You need to learn a bit about leisure. Why don't you come with me Sunday morning for some racquetball. We used to play all the time before I became supervisor." Richard said.

"You know, Rich. That's the best offer I've had in ages. Is that club still open near your house?" Carl queried.

"Sure is. You might be surprised to know that Tracy, the cashier there owns the place now." On hearing Rich say the word "owns" Carl felt a tinge of sadness. There was so many things he could have done with his life, so many places he had gone if he hadn't had to spend the last 10 years of his wife's life and all their savings just taking care of her. Alzheimers was a cruel bitch. Despite the unpleasant feeling that came with thinking of his wife and her final days, Carl thought to himself that it would be good to see Tracy again.

"Okay then," Carl said, "Make us a booking for 10am on Sunday and you'll see what one of us old guys can do."

"You're on, Carl. Talk to you then." Came Richard's reply.

****

Carl spent most of Saturday thinking about the match-up. Firstly he had thought back to his younger days when he would get books about racquetball that showed him strategy, showed him how to condition himself and how to practise. During that Saturday he stood for half an hour practising his backhand, his fore-hand, his smash and his serve with an old racquet he had sitting until he eventually knocked a lamp off its' stand and then took a walk down to a mall near his apartment to see what the new racquetball racquets were like. Some of them were pretty snazzy. Strong, light, colourful. It cost him a little over $60.00, but he bought one that just looked undefeatable. Carl had a hard time sleeping, but eventually he drifted off and got his 8 hours in, more than he needed.

At 9:30am at the racquet club Carl went in and asked for Tracy and sadly it turned out that it was Tracy he had asked. He had no idea she would look so old, even though Carl himself had grown a few grey hairs and added a few wrinkles. He wasn't going to let the mistake spoil his fun though, and he went at the game full bore. By the end of the hour they had booked for the court, he was sweating profusely and barely able to keep his breath. For the next few working days he was incredibly sore, but it all felt worth it to 'get back in the game' so to speak. Carl and Richard played more over the next few weeks, and when Carl was in a bit better shape, Richard decided he was ready for the next level.

"Carl, " Richard said to him over the beers they had after each match. "Why don't you come hunting with me next long weekend up in the bush near my cabin? I haven't gone in a while, it's a nice place and it would feel good to get some exercise out of doors."

"I don't see why not. I don't have a rifle anymore, though. Lucy made me get rid of mine years ago." Carl said, feeling quite honoured that his old friend had now once again gained respect for him. "And if I'm going to use your rifle, we should hit the shooting range before we go."

"Yeah, that sounds good. You pay for the range and the ammunition and I'll cover the cost of the hunting license and of course provide the cabin." Richard replied.

Carl was starting for the first time since his wife had died to feel like a happy and participating member of the human race. It was a funny feeling, but somewhere in the back of his head he had another feeling, one that kind of bothered him a bit but he couldn't tell why. All he really knew was that he loved hunting, loved shooting and he had given both up many years ago.

****

When time came for Richard and Carl to head out to Richard's cabin there was still quite a bit of snow on the ground, but in Carl's mind that only served to make things appear more beautiful. They didn't talk much in the three and a half hours it took to get to Richard's cabin, it was like they were both mesmerized at the task at hand, the beauty of the Northern Canadian land around them as they drove, and a small feeling of anticipation and a sense of danger. Richard was the first one to speak.

"Carl, did you ever hear me talk about the red wolf?" Richard asked.

"Not that I can remember." Came Carl's reply.

"Well, last time I came up to the cabin a trapper was coming through, a native fellow, and I had him in for a coffee and some beans and pork. He was telling me that there used to be a legend about a wolf near the area the cabin is in that was seen but not caught, was the leader of any pack he ran with, was bigger and stronger and somehow had avoided hunters all his life. What do you make of something like that?"

"I think that's the kind of thing a local makes up to keep hunters and their money coming back for year after year." Carl joked.

"Could be, but sometimes at night in the cabin you can hear these wolf cries and it gives me the creeps. I get this impression that this wolf protects the deer and animals up there. I have to be honest with you, I invited you because I don't like hunting alone up there anymore."

"Well, whatever makes you feel better." Carl said, without taking his eyes off the trees and valleys and blue blue skies.

****

On the third day of their trip, the two hunters had yet to find the elusive deer they had sought. They had had more than their share of fun though, they fooled around tossing cans in the air trying to shoot them out of their arc, they had knocked back beer and whiskey each night until they both became quite open and talkative, but the goal, the reason for Carl feeling renewed by coming up to the woods hadn't occurred. They had not killed anything.

But then, at about two in the afternoon, the two of them spotted some fresh deer tracks and scat. It would take some time, and it would take them a long way out of their way but with that much, the two, having had experience galore from hunting trips dating all the way back to their teen years, could get this animal. Carl's heart started pounding faster at just the thought of it.

For two hours Richard and Carl stealthily followed the deer tracks, sometimes circling in case the animal was close to avoid the creature catching their smell, these were skittish animals. Then, as the day had worn on to four thirty, there stood the magnificent mammal, totally unaware that its life was about to end. Carl had spotted the deer first, so he was given first shot. First the two of them lay prone and Richard took out his binoculars and estimated the distance of the shot. Then Carl tuned in his rifle scope and cautiously, carefully squared off the deer in his sights. He was so excited that as he pulled the trigger all he could see was a flash of something moving quickly in front of the creature at the very moment his shot rang out. The deer bolted, making Carl curse all things in heaven and earth, but there was still something there where the deer had stood.

The two hunters trudged up to where the shot would have connected with their prey, and there lying on the ground and bleeding was a wolf. Not just any wolf, it was a wolf with a streak of red on his back.

"Damn, that deer would have been nice, but look what we got by accident." Carl exclaimed, quite happy with the outcome.

"Accident? I don't know this was an accident, Carl. How does a wolf jump in front of a bullet and get shot by accident?" Richard said, a bit fearfully.

"Oh, does it really matter? This wolf is dead and we can stuff it or sell the hide. This is way better than a deer." Carl boasted. "Oh, wait a minute. He's still alive." Carl said, then turned the self-sacrificing wolf over to see his face. He looked into his eyes, and all at once something very strange happened. It was sort of like being injected with a half a gallon of whiskey that had fermented so long it made you hallucinate. For a brief flash of a moment, Carl felt some force, some spirit rushing into him, strengthening him, all over and throughout ever pore and fibre of his body. It was both rapture and sickness, pain and pleasure, glory and shame. It ended just as quickly as it had began, and when it ended, Carl literally fell over backwards and didn't move after he landed.

"Carl! Carl!" Richard yelled, not getting any answer. "Carl, are you okay? What's going on?" Richard reacted quickly, checking for heart rate, breathing, everything. He assumed Carl was having a heart attack, and he wasn't far off. With the motivation that comes from the possible loss of a close friend, Richard went to work and managed to get Carl breathing within a few seconds and when he seemed a bit stable, pulled out his cell phone and ran to the top of a nearby hill to get a signal and call for help. As he was doing this, as help was on the way, Carl lay there with a tiny Buddha-like smile on his face, just as though he had come to some new level of awareness and tranquility.

****

Help came, and the Doctors that saw Carl were a bit baffled, but soon sent him home, and after a few weeks of convalescence, Carl felt good enough to go back to work. In all the excitement of his heart attack, they didn't retrieve the carcass of the wolf Carl had killed. The days went by and after a few months, Carl even resumed playing racquetball and became quite good at it. Once the initial shock wore off and he resumed a normal life, he became quite a changed man. He worked twice as hard, he often even stayed late to complete tasks and despite his age and circumstance, when his hunting partner Richard took his early retirement, Carl took over his supervisory position. Little did Carl know it came with nearly double his former salary and a company car. Before long, Carl had saved an bought a comfortable house in the arts district, and began seeing a 30 year-old woman with whom he went on long jogs with and played tennis and various sports with. The new friends he had acquired thought he was headed for an early grave with the pace he kept, but on he went.

Carl became very ambitious and when he reached the mandatory retirement age of 65 he simply walked out on his last day with a memory stick with all the client lists and other sensitive materials he could steal and he went off and started his own company. For seven years humble Carl lived as lavishly and comfortably as anyone could ask for and no longer found himself needing to risk his livelihood to play a childish video game. His game was acquisitions, and his company grew.

One day in the life of Carl's new company he had made a gambit to partner up with one of his strongest rivals only the stipulation was made that he carry insurance enough so that should anything happen his new partner would be covered. The insurance would have been no problem, despite what seemed ludicrous terms of payments, but the company stipulated he must take a medical before it would go into effect. There was no doubting when the results came back, our infallible and adventurous Carl had pancreatic Cancer, and one thing he didn't have was time (or an insurance policy). It was estimated he would live 3 months at the most, his particular affliction was Cancer that was pretty much untreatable.

After going through the motions of second opinions, and miracle-promising quacks that advertise in pop-up ads on the Internet, Carl liquidated his assets, gave a good chunk to his girlfriend, and purchased Richard's old cabin. It would have been nice to have his old friend with him, but Richard had long since passed into the great beyond.

With barely more than a 50-word note and a few phone calls to family he had long since given up on, Carl loaded up a pick-up with a canopy over the box, and headed North the three and half hours to where he had not been since he was a humble employee of men who now kissed his feet. It was more than ten years, and Carl could not help but feel in some way that he was going home.

Along with his rifle and some books and some sparse creature comforts along with two months' supply of food, Carl was on his way to run out the clock in the only place that had ever really given him anything he could use.

It took just about all the time and all the food he had to do it, but one day many miles away from his cabin, Carl found wolf tracks. Near them he built a simple shelter from his poncho and lit a fire and sat down to wait.

Not long after dark, Carl heard the sad howl of the lone timber-wolf. It could have been one of a million of the same creature, but somehow Carl knew which wolf this howl belonged to. When he heard it, he scrambled to his feet, walked up a hill and despite how strange it seemed, he reached down deep inside himself and began to howl at the moon. The wolf off in the distance, to his surprise, would howl, then Carl would howl back. This went on for nearly an hour. As that time went past, Carl could feel his heart beat faster. Not from fear or anticipation, but from some kind of animal instinct he carried deep within him. A few things happened to our friend Carl. His night vision and sense of smell grew exponentially. His muscles strengthened without growing or changing. He became a wolf, not just any wolf, Carl became a Red Wolf and he howled out all the pain and emotion and sadness and even happiness that collect in one's soul over seventy-plus years. And he could understand the cries of the other wolf, who had roamed these hills and valleys for at least ten times that amount of years.

After the exchange of mutual respect and wolf cries, Carl felt as though everything had been completed, everything but one simple act. He sat down and looked over the trees and the grasses and the moon and stars, all the beautiful things that God had given him and his last companion on earth. It seemed perfectly normal to him, his pain rose substantially and so he laid down right where he was and embraced the pain. He had taken no painkillers, he used no special methods. He just accepted that his pain was part of life, his end was part of life. He lay there for perhaps a half an hour, dreaming of his wife, thinking of the children he never had and the niece he hadn't spoken to in years. Then, there was the Red Wolf, calm and gentle as a kitten, sniffing at Carl, poking at him with his muscular feet. Finally the Red Wolf turned Carl over, and as he drew his last breath, the wolf looked into Carl's eyes and Carl's soul slipped into the wolf's soul and both were again at peace.

THE END

Leif Gregersen

WWW.666.COM

    The 17 year-old, slightly obese young man sat quite comfortably in his reclining chair in the basement of his mother's house. As he could be found most of the time, he was seated in front of a three-screen display powered by a computer that had more to it than its' outside case implied. This machine the young boy could nimbly manipulate as keys whirred and mouse clicked had the latest and greatest parts from processor to RAM to its multiple video cards and externally attached Terabyte hard drives of which there were four. Any movie he wanted to watch, any game he wanted to play, any supermodel he wanted to see naked was right at his fingertips, at lightning speed and in high definition.

    Oftentimes the boy, whose name was Sheldon, would immerse himself in a world of magic and witchcraft by watching a marathon of movies or even documentaries on the subject he was interested in. Then he would cut loose in one of his cracked games that would provide the most realistic simulation to the stories that would whisk him off to his fantasy worlds. When he could tear himself away from the computer for long enough there would be books, ordered on-line to an untraceable address which would be paid for with stolen credit card numbers, the same ones that supplied his growing need for faster and larger and newer parts for his joy machine. There was nothing he could not do with his machine, from cracking business websites for information he needed to steal people's identity, or getting into the games he basically stole from file-sharing sites in order to make the music and the graphics more hard-core, more violent.

Today, however, Sheldon was after something he didn't often seek out, today Sheldon was looking for revenge. Earlier that week a now former friend had called him a loser and a geek and now he was going to pay for his words. Our 'hero' had cracked his new enemies' service provider and had been stalking him for two days now, looking for a chance to strike back, now he was close to having it. Sheldon's former friend was now in a chat room, and, using multiple windows, he was going to hit the poor guy where it hurt. He started out by logging in using the name Darlene, and it went something like this:

Darlene: Hey-asl? (asl-age, sex, location)

Dan :23 (lie), male, Edmonton.

Darlene: I'm 19 and I'm also from Edmonton, way on the South end of town.

Dan: What do you look like?

Darlene: 109 pounds, slim, with long brown hair. I broke up with my boyfriend 2 weeks ago, he

couldn't keep up with me in bed.

Dan: I'll bet I could keep up with you.

Darlene: What makes you say that? What do you look like?

Dan: I'm 5'10", got six-pack abs and my Dad's hard-on pills. I can go for hours.

Darlene: Do you have condoms?

Dan: Yeah, why?

Darlene: Meet me at the Echoes Restaurant on 23rd avenue in Millwoods.

Dan: When?

Darlene: As soon as you can get there, but you have to bring flowers, a dozen roses.

Dan: Why?

Darlene: So I know who you are, plus it's a tradition.

Dan: I'll be there in half an hour.

With that transmission, Sheldon snickered to himself and thought of this dumb ass sitting in a restaurant for the next four hours thinking he's a stud. That part about needing his Dad's hard-on pills would make good gossip for the group they hung out in. What Sheldon didn't see was the url that appeared on the screen after he logged off the chat site, it read: www.666.com Sheldon didn't click on it which was unfortunate, but he would run across it again soon enough.

****

It would have been nice to go out to the Echoes Restaurant just to piss off Dan, but Sheldon had a rule that when he got revenge, he would be the last person to be suspected of giving it, which had kept him out of many a beating in the past. The day rolled on and in the morning

Sheldon's mom asked him to mail a letter for her, so he set out to walk the 4 blocks to drop the letter off for her. It certainly seemed simple enough, open the box, drop in the letter, go back home and smoke a joint and watch some trippy movie for a while. When he got to the box though, Sheldon opened the chute and a loud, loud 'bang' greeted him along with a cloud of smoke. Nearly scared the shit out of him, then when he looked inside, someone had printed the same url again, this time with a shaky hand. It read, just as before, www.666.com. He should have been pissed off, and he would normally be trying to figure out what to do to whoever had set up this gag, but for whatever reason it kind of made him chuckle. All of a sudden now he could think of a dozen places that would be great to hide a firecracker like this. Obviously, Sheldon thought to himself, this website has some nasty virus on it.

When he got home Sheldon called up one of his friends that he liked even less than Dan, though this other friend, Michael, didn't know this. Mike was always inviting Sheldon to his birthday parties and offering to lend him things. He was pretty annoying but Sheldon always went to the parties because of the wanton way Mike's entire overweight family consumed the best of foods, from their daily steaks or pizzas, to the double chocolate caramel sundaes they passed out whenever anything special happened.

Sheldon got to Mike's house within the hour and asked Mike if he wanted to see something cool on the computer. Mike agreed, and Sheldon, not caring that Mike's parents had spent over $2,000.00 to buy this computer for their unfortunate son, typed in the url www.666.com without even thinking first. The site came up and it didn't seem harmful at all. In actuality, it had all kinds of cool links. It had download icons where you could get classic games from older computer systems and arcades, it had free streaming television, millions of music files and basically everything a hacker could want in an underground website. There was even a link to a shady publisher who printed books on hacking and of course, books on how to get revenge, perhaps Sheldon's favourite topic. He had heard of this stuff, but due to recent crackdowns, most of these sites had been shut down. The only thing that really sucked about it was that you had to have a credit card or mail them a money order before you could do anything. Without exposing too much, Sheldon shut the computer down and asked Mike if his mom had sundae fixings in the house. She did, and the pair gorged themselves then Sheldon made excuses not to stay longer with his eager friend and headed for home.

****

When Sheldon got home he dug up an older laptop that he kept around for situations like the one he was in right now. He really wanted to get into the information on this site, but he had to do it without being traced, without using a stolen credit card. There had to be a way. The first thing he came up with was an old hacker's trick. He started out by scanning his wireless modem program to see if there were any open networks transmitting near him. By luck there was, an unnamed source that was not password protected. "Excellent!" Sheldon said out loud,

The Base Jumpers and Other Stories

on learning that the hardest step was now complete. Next, he called up the website www.666.com and clicked on a link to register a membership. He started with the dumbest name he could think of, john3:16. After he typed this in and hit return, the page he was on refreshed and a message popped up in red saying this name had been taken. This was just about all he needed. He logged out of the site.

Within a few moments, Sheldon logged back in to the site and this time clicked the link to log in, instead of to register. He typed in 'John3:16' for username and then under password tried the following:

God, enter, and the response came: password incorrect

Love, enter, password incorrect

Love3:16, enter, password incorrect, one more try the message came

GodisLove, enter, welcome John! He was in.

Sheldon laughed at the sheer simplicity of this, old tricks like this hadn't worked in years for him, but today he was rolling all six's for some reason. He logged off and powered up his main computer and went back to the website. There was no worry now about being traced, he would crack their security and make himself a full member with unlimited download credits. What could they do? They were software pirates, the most that could happen would be for them to shut down his account.

For the next three hours Sheldon ran every type of software he could, all the password generators, everything. Nothing brought forth any fruit. It was nearing 3am and he had been up for way too long and been way to excited to keep up with all this tedious work, so he closed the Internet browser window and was about to leave his chair when another idea hit him that he hadn't tried. He logged in, under username typed in 'admin' and then 'root' and the computer replied with the words, "Administrator powers now active." Suddenly the adrenaline rushed into him and he went a little power mad. He started downloading music first of all, then scanned through the classic games they had in this amazing little site, then he went deeper.

It took a while for all his songs to download, this place had the best speed metal he had heard in a long time and after a joint, waves of ecstatic pleasure rolled over him. As he sat revelling in the music and feeling of power he had of breaking into such a place, Sheldon found something a little out of the ordinary. It was a link to a game, and it didn't seem to be complete. He clicked on the link and it took him to a page that had a strong warning: "This game is full of violence and carnage and is intended for adults only, preferably those who are experienced gamers. Use at your own risk."

There was no way Sheldon could resist after seeing that. He checked the movement keys, which were normal for a 3-D shoot-em-up and clicked on the link to start the game, then selected the option on the next screen that read, "Playing in super 3-D, like no other game." He smiled, took a toke of his joint, put it down and prepared to be sucked into something he had never seen, never done, this was all new territory for him.

****

It was hard to say how long it took to find Sheldon. All they really know was that there was a fire, a terrible one. It seemed to have started from downstairs, possibly from a frayed computer cord or some kind of microchip that had been over-clocked so many times it had caught fire. For the first little while, Sheldon's mom had hoped against hope that her boy had gotten out and would turn up at a friend's house or something. When she called her ex-husband to tell him about the fire she talked so strangely that it was as if Sheldon was most certainly alive, although by this point, even a true believer would admit there was very little chance of that. When the fire inspectors cleared the wreckage it seemed somehow that Sheldon had experienced so much heat in such a short space of time that his shoes had melted to the floor and he had been mummified. When they tried to explain this to his mother, all she was heard to say was,

"Damn it! I had told that boy a thousand times not to wear his shoes in the house."

He had been a bad boy, though shoes in the house wasn't the worst of it. All that was really known was that the strange website Sheldon's friend Micheal told the police about was never found again, and no record of such a site had ever been registered. Just like Sheldon, www.666.com was gone forever.

Leif Gregersen

A MILLION TO ONE

The middle-aged man stood on the Skytrain Platform holding a folded newspaper page in one hand and writing numbers down in a notebook he held with the newspaper with his other hand. He seemed just about totally oblivious to the milling crowd around him. If he looked up from what he was doing he would be able to see across Vancouver Harbour and take in the beauty of the mountains that marked the North Side of the renowned city. He might have also have been able to strike up a conversation with some of his fellow train riders, especially since he had ridden this particular train at this time as he waited on this spot pretty much since it had been built. There were all kinds of people who recognized him, but something about the attitude of the big city made people often less friendly than smaller ones would be. Day after day, year after year, the numbers man made few connections with anyone.

His name was Art, and he was off to his job as a bookkeeper for a medium-sized clothing store not far off Granville Street. When the time came to get on the train, Art was neither pushy nor overly polite. He had grown up in Vancouver and had seen it grow with almost total indifference. He was not a terribly noticeable guy, and he wasn't much of a dresser, which is perhaps why we find him here on the train, his eyes darting from his paper to his notebook and back again, a single, 47 year-old with no dependants and no wife or girlfriend.

Art crossed Granville and headed off towards his work and stopped at a convenience store for a one cream, one sugar cup of coffee and when he got to the counter to pay he handed over a filled-in lottery slip, paid for his items, neatly folded his ticket and put it away in his wallet and walked on to work.

It was Saturday when the mystery was finally solved. Art was at home, watching television after another restless night of half-sleep, half wakefulness, and he heard the paper thump at the door. He went out and a shock went through him when he read the headline. It said: "Winning Lottery Jackpot Still Not Claimed." This had happened a hundred times over the years but for some reason this time when he saw it, Art had a funny feeling. He raced over to where he kept his old papers and opened the Wednesday edition to where they printed the numbers. Then he took out his wallet somehow knowing what had happened. He didn't need to read the numbers, but he did, over and over. There they were, all six numbers. It shocked him, but then he thought of how many printing mistakes the paper made and how long the odds were to win Three Million Dollars, so he quickly dressed and walked down to the corner store that had a ticket checker.

When he got there, he had a hard time concealing his excitement, thinking about all the years he had faithfully taken all the winning numbers twice a week and applied calculations he had heard about, read about and even some he invented for this purpose in the hopes that one day this dream could come true. He handed the clerk the ticket without letting on what he thought, other than a simple query to see if the ticket was a winner as he had often done before.

The clerk took the ticket to the lottery machine at the far end of the counter and seemed to take quite a while. He ran it through a couple of times then came back and handed a ticket back to Art and said he was sorry, that the ticket hadn't won. Art let out a long sigh and realized that yes, it was too good to be true and was about to scrunch up the ticket and throw it away but he stopped to look at it first.

"Hey, wait a minute! This isn't my ticket!"

"That's the ticket you gave me." Replied the clerk.

"No, no, I'm not stupid. I deal with numbers all the time. And this isn't my kind of pencil either. I use a number two. This is not my ticket. Give me back my damn ticket!"

"Are you okay pal? You look a little shook up. You made a mistake, that's all. Happens all the time!"

"What the hell do you mean I made a mistake! I DON'T MAKE MISTAKES!"

"Hey, if you're going to get loud, you're going to have to leave!"

"I'll leave alright, but I'm going to be back with the police!" Art declared as he stormed outside to a payphone. As he was dialing the phone he could see in the store and the clerk had come out from behind the counter and started to run to the back door. "Hey!" Art yelled as he came back in the front door. "Hey, stop!"

Art ran him down and tackled him and managed to get the ticket out of the guy's hand and told him: "Tried to steal it eh! Well, I have news for you. If you had just helped me get it to the BC Lotto office you would have gotten a bonus, now you get nothing!" With that, Art walked out, called a cab and said nothing after he sat down in the back seat though his mind was racing. He took the cab to the Lottery office and in a few short hours and with a bit of celebrating and a few photos, Art was BC's newest millionaire.

//////////////////////////////////

Days and weeks passed and Art found himself in all kinds of places. In Japan he paid $300.00 for a steak that had been raised on beer and massages. In Korea he discovered a million and one more uses for cabbage. In Thailand he went to a strip joint that at one point asked for volunteers from the audience. After a while he began to miss his Native Vancouver, but decided to visit Australia before he returned. There it seemed, everything revolved around beer. It was a beautiful country and the people were fantastic but they partied at a pace that was beyond him. In the last couple of days of his trip, he decided he had spent too much, even though it was a pittance compared to what he had won, and consulted with a few specialists in investments in Melbourne before going back home.

After returning to Vancouver, Art soon found that it was no longer the same to him. Not even bothering to rent a house, he got a room in a motel with a kitchenette within walking distance of the train. Everything seemed so dirty and dog eat dog so Art went and took a couple of courses in coastal navigation, and made plans to head to Mexico and live on a small yacht until he got tired of it. Other than flying over it he didn't know much about the sea. He had, of course, gone on the ferries to Victoria but that was far from what he wanted to do now. He applied himself studiously to the classes and read as much as he could about the subject and before long he was ready to leave once again.

Art spent the next few days looking at small yachts and capping off his evenings reading US newspapers and drinking just enough to put himself to sleep. One day he walked into a restaurant in a small coastal town he had spent a bit of time in and there was the most beautiful young woman he had ever seen. She wasn't young but wasn't old and stale either. She had shoulder length dark Hispanic hair with a shock of grey in it and looked like she really took care of herself. Her skin was radiant and her eyes seemed to glow with beauty and sexual magnetism. He caught himself staring at her and then reminded himself what he was there to do. He had the phone numbers of a couple of ads he had seen and called them to enquire only to find out they had both been sold. He decided to sit down for a beer to cool himself off a bit and to his surprise, the beautiful woman spoke to him.

"Excuse me Mister Americano. I understand you are looking for a boat."

"Well, you are right and wrong. I am actually a Canadian and yes I am looking for a boat, a sailboat to be exact, no less than 20 feet."

"My brother has such a boat! Would you like to see it? I can take you there." Art was a little suspicious, but the thought of getting to know this woman and maybe even finding a boat made the offer pretty appealing, appealing enough for him to lower his guard.

It turned out the boat was in pretty good shape and after inspecting it and checking for safety equipment, Art made the decision to buy. The young woman he had met, Elithia, turned out to be quite friendly as well. It seemed to take no effort to ask her to join him and help him get his sea legs. After a few days of cautiously sailing and testing everything on his new acquisition, Art brought the boat to a shipwright for final fitting and fixing to prepare for him to move on down the coastline. He checked into a hotel and Elithia came with him. For the next few days he experienced lovemaking like he never imagined it could be, this woman was in her prime and had few inhibitions. One night after a session they sat on the balcony of their room, barely clothed but not ashamed of each other. They talked on a long time, and perhaps even to his surprise, Art asked her if she would like to travel with him.

"I can not go. I have no money. My family is everything to me."

"Well, there is a way you and I can be family. And you might say I'm in a position that if we did, if we got married that is, we wouldn't have to ever worry about money."

"What do you mean? I thought you were a bookkeeper from Vancouver and all you had was that boat."

"I don't want to get into it. Let's just say I can support us."

"You really want to get married?"

"Yes, honestly. And I will love, honor and obey. I don't take promises lightly."

Somehow at that moment the moonlight revealed Elithia's radiant beauty and a sort of peace and happiness communicated to him through her smile. He half didn't know what he was doing, but Art leaned in and kissed her lips and then held her and they both cried tears of joy. For the very first time in his life Art felt deeply for another human being. He had his dream now, the dream of being far away and out of the world that had kept him stuck in one rut, one course, and that would still have him to this day if he hadn't taken a chance.

////////////////////////

When the boat was ready, Elithia went home alone to pack and Art made a few taxi trips back and forth to where his boat now was in temporary moorings . The plan was to spend one last night at the hotel and then say goodbye to everything and set sail before either of them changed their minds.

On this particular night Art had brought a ring, a rather nice one, with a diamond solitaire set in yellow gold. He also brought champagne, of a selection so expensive that it has more of an effect of making one 'high' than drunk. They began the evening with a few drinks and soon fell into passionate embraces of lovemaking. When the had completed their bedroom adventures, Art went on about where he wanted to go, what he wanted to see, and they both drank and fell asleep in each other's arms. A few hours after dark they were rudely awakened by the smashing of their hotel room door being kicked open.

"What are you doing you filthy whore!" The overweight Mexican figure yelled as he pulled Elithia from the bed. "You were supposed to distract him not fuck him!"

"Hey what the hell are you doing!" Art answered, completely confused.

"If you want to stay alive my Americano friend you will shut up and do as you are told." The Mexican giant replied, pulling back his thin jean jacket to reveal a pistol still in its holster.

"Elithia, who the hell is this?" Art asked, in an exasperated tone.

"This is my brother's partner!" Elithia replied, tears forming in her eyes as she spoke. "He wants to steal your money."

"Money! What money? What do you want?"

"You made a withdrawl today, my friend. You took money from your bank and put it on my boat. But you are a smart man. You had the combination changed. Now you will tell me the new combination or you will die."

"He's serious Arthur. He has done this many times." By now Elithia was weeping heavily.

"Go ahead, kill me. You won't get away with it and it won't get you the combination. When I don't arrive at my destination you will be found, and I don't think Mexican jails are as nice as the ones we Americanos have." Art was bluffing, he didn't want to die, and no one would miss him if he did. All he was doing was trying to buy time.

"Get your clothes on, my friend. I want to take you somewhere." With a bit of minor violence and some coaching, They managed to get Art into their van and blindfolded him. Elithia they left behind. It wasn't a long drive, but it was long enough for Art to run a thousand grisly scenarios through his head. How could Elithia have done this? Did she have any choice? Would these people really kill him? He was practically shaking with fear and extreme anxiety. How had he gotten this far from home and knee deep in shit?

When they got to the isolated shack they called home, Art was taken inside still blindfolded and was tied to a chair securely. They took off the blindfold and all he could see was a couple of dark looking characters and a case of pop near a couple of stained old army cots.

"Do you know why we have these my Americano friend?" The larger of the two asked Art, pointing to the pop bottles.

"Having a party afterwards?" He replied.

"No, this is a special surprise just for you. Did you know that once a prison riot was willingly stopped by inmates in a Mexico city prison just by a show of a truckload of soda such as these?"

"No, I didn't know. Maybe you have to explain."

"I will do better my friend, I am going to demonstrate. And after I demonstrate you will give me the new safe combination." With that, the smaller of the two henchmen took Art's head and tied it back all the way so he was nearly looking up at the ceiling. Then asshole number one took out a pop, opened it, took a sip, then put his thumb securely in the bottle and shook it up. What happened next, Art was ill prepared for. He sprayed the high-pressure liquid right up his nose and the carbonated, shooting stream of angry liquid shot seemingly right into his brain. The pain was so intense and complete that all he could do was scream.

"Stop! Stop! Stop!" The pain didn't end with the end of the pop, it seemed to eat away at his sinuses and nasal cavity, as though all the inside of his head was burning. "Fuck! I'll tell you. Have the fucking money!"

"Well, you know that is all we wanted to hear. We want you to know we are not murderers, but we have many friends. You tell us the combination, we get the money and you never come back to this part of the world again. You can go back to America, or wherever. Just don't come back here. Can you agree with that?"

"Yes, yes!" Art yelled, still in excruciating pain.

"Good, now what is the combination?"

"Four, twenty-three, seventeen."

"Are you sure? You know I can go check and come back. But if you tell the truth, my partner will let you go when I have the money."

"Yes! FUCK! I'm sure! I don't lie. I wouldn't lie. Just don't do that again!"

"Well, that is the sad part. Always when I seal a deal with someone they get the idea they can fool me. So I will just give you one more spray and then I will go get the money and you can go."

"No, No! No!" Art screamed through the blinding haze of pain that was about to go tenfold again. When it ended, the torment slowly subsided and Art started to feel he would survive, he would live. Things would be tough without his money but he would get through. The bastard may even take his passport so he had to return to Canada but he would live with that too. In a few hours he would be out on the open sea and all this would be behind him, the only real pain was that he would likely never see Elithia again, either she was in on it and she had faked everything, or she was forced to do it and would just wait around for the next victim with a lonely face and a big wallet. Within the next couple of hours a phone rang in the shack and after a short conversation the armed desperado released him and drove him blindfolded to the docks. Art got on his boat and motored out of the harbour, then set sail for Vancouver. The game was over and he had lost, but he still had some pride left.

/////////////////////////////

A few weeks later at a Motel Art was sitting and watching TV when a knock came at his door. He looked through the viewer and there was a young woman standing outside with blonde hair and carrying a briefcase. He didn't know anyone knew he was there but when he heard the voice on the other side a chill went through him. Still, he opened the door.

"Elithia? What are you doing here?" He asked.

"I... I... I'm sorry. I don't know what to say. I told the consulate I had to return this to you and with a little bribe they told me you were staying here. I have your passport... and this." She handed him the briefcase and he noticed that she was wearing the ring he had bought for her. Art opened the briefcase and there it was, all the money (just about) that was stolen. "I don't know if you want me anymore. I don't know if you can ever trust me. I just wanted to come here to say I do love you. You are kind and honest and my brother and those men were monsters. I took that money from them and now it's yours again. I realized money can't help anyone when they are bad inside and that when I was with you I always felt good and I didn't lie or fake anything." With that she broke down and started crying again.

"Come in, come in. Elithia! I love you too! And I do trust you. I do want to marry you. Don't worry about going back to Mexico and those men finding you. I was only waiting for my passport so I could go to Australia and build a life for myself that I can stomach. I'm so glad you came back. Only you didn't have to steal my money back, that money didn't matter."

"How could all that money not matter? We were going to use it to start over. Now we can. We might have to work very hard but we will be together. We can be together and I can be away from those bastards."

"Elithia, I have something to tell you. Besides that I love you."

"What? Is anything wrong?"

"No, things are fantastic!" Art exclaimed as he gripped his love tightly. "I just want to tell you that when I said I was well off enough not to worry, I wasn't just talking about what I had in that Mexican bank that I put on the boat. I didn't want to let on that..." Art stopped himself.

"What? How could twenty thousand dollars not matter to someone?"

"Let's just say I locked away a few bonds when I was in Australia."

THE THINGS WE DO FOR MONEY

"So you're saying nothing can go wrong?" Rob asked Morris, the man he had been drinking with in the skid row hotel bar for the past three hours.

"No, not a thing. First, I get you the pistol. For that, you owe me 25% of what you get. Then the next morning at ten o'clock you go to the North End Credit Union Bank, put the nylon over your face, walk in, fire off two rounds and pass around the bag to be filled with cash. Say as little as possible, then walk out and my guy, who will expect $300 for the favor, will pick you up in his cab and take you wherever. Then you just lay low and in a couple of days I'll come buy for my cut and to pick up the gun and we're done."

"It can't be that easy!" Rob said as he maneuvered the little video game icon around the maze of the game table they sat at."

"Well the trick is you use a gun that can't be traced, you cover your face and don't leave any prints. And don't get greedy. If they give you $1,000.00, take it, don't go around threatening people for more or looking to go into the safe. Just get in and get out. Come see me here tomorrow at closing and I'll give you the gun. But for now, I have to run. Don't drink too much the night before you pull this one, you need a clear head." Morris got up and drained his beer, and left a twenty for the tab. As he got up, Rob went to smile and shake his hand which kind of made Morris feel a bit funny about this kid. Any normal tough guy would just grunt or go on with his game. Rob here actually looked like he was trying to impress him. Oh well, as long as I get my cut I don't care how stupid this kid is, he thought.

Rob sat in the bar and ordered glasses of draft beer until the twenty and his own ten bucks were gone. Then he paid the tab and went upstairs to the small room he had been renting above this run-down, 100 year-old Hotel in the middle of Edmonton's Inner City. He laid there for a while enjoying the buzz the beer had gave him, smoking hand-rolled cigarettes and thinking about what he was going to do with all the money he would get. It all seemed like a dream come true, he had been half joking in the bar when he said to a guy he was at the end of his rope and would do anything for some money or a job. It seemed like good luck he had met Morris who was setting all of this up for him. He didn't remember falling asleep but he dreamed of finally getting out of the city after doing just one more thing with the bank job money. One more thing.

///////////////////////////

"Okay Rob, just let me get this through to you. I need this gun back." Morris said, and slipped the pistol wrapped in a 'free' newspaper which Rob slipped into his belt. "Tomorrow you get up early, take the 154 bus to the North End, get off near the bank. Then at ten o'clock you walk in, fire off two rounds and toss your gym bag or a garbage bag or whatever you have over the counter and tell them to fill it up with cash. Remember: don't get greedy! Then go out and get into the waiting cab and just casually tell him where you want to go and when you get there give him $300 and that's that. Get rid of the bag you used first and your jacket, buy new ones and then go check in to room 25 at the York on the other side of town. I'll be along to collect my cut and the gun in a few days when the heat dies down. Got all that?"

"Get a bag, take the 154 Northbound bus, go in the bank at ten, fire off two rounds and then get the money together and get into the cab waiting outside. Get a new jacket and a new bag, pay the driver, and check in to room 25 at the York. Okay?"

"Sounds like you've got it. Now if you get a good chunk of money don't go crazy. Make it last, don't leave yourself desperate and have to do another job and get sloppy. I think you can pull this off, just keep your head on your shoulders and don't fuck up." With that, Morris walked away and didn't shake Rob's hand that had been extended. Rob didn't care, he liked the thrill that having a loaded gun with him gave him. Before he went to bed that night he had just one more thing to do.

"Hello Operator?" Rob spoke into the payphone handset. "Do you have a listing for a Benjamin Donner in Edmonton?"

"I have a listing for a B. Donner but it's unlisted." Fuck! Rob thought. What was that trick some guy taught me... oh yeah, I remember.

"Is that the one on 24 Maple Crescent?" Rob asked.

"No, this one is on 15 Dunvegan."

"Oh, that wouldn't be it then, thanks." Rob wrote down 15 Dunvegan on his pocket address book's back page and then phoned the city to find out which bus would take him there. After catching the bus it only took twenty five or thirty minutes to get to the affluent neighborhood and he soon found Ben's house. Trying not to look like he had a gun stuffed in his waist, Rob walked up to the door and knocked. Someone came to the door quickly. It was him.

"Can I help you?" Benjamin Donner said as he opened the door and looked at Rob's shabby clothes and unshaven face.

"I don't know-do you know how to die?" Rob said and pointed the gun at Benjamin Donner's head.

"W..w..who the hell are you?" He stammered.

"Maybe you don't remember me but I remember you throwing me over a fence in grade ten and me hurting my back so bad it still goes out of whack now and then. Well Ben buddy, it's payback time."

"You're not going to shoot me." Benjamin said, sounding more calm.

"What makes you think that?"

"Because the safety is on. You don't even know how to shoot a fucking gun, numb nuts." Numb nuts. That old insult. The bastard did remember him. Rob wasn't sure which was the safety, but he felt a switch near his thumb so he clicked it down and the magazine that held the bullets for the automatic fell right out. "Ha ha! You dumb asshole, you don't know how to shoot a gun. Now get the hell off my property before I kick your ass and call the police." Rob felt like a total idiot, and he took the pistol down from aiming it at Benjamin and had a look at it. He noticed the switch that was the safety and clicked it back, then pulled back the hammer with his thumb. He had really just wanted to scare his former bully but with all the anger and hate inside of him he now really wanted to kill him, but before he could pick up the magazine that held the bullets, Benjamin kicked his gun hand away from him but the gun went off with a loud 'crack!!!'

"Shit, you were going to..." Benjamin went white. The bullet had lodged in his front door, there must have been one in the chamber. He pushed Rob back, slammed the door in his face and ran inside to call the police. Rob picked up the magazine and ran away as fast as he could, but in just two or three short minutes he could hear sirens. He ended up running down an alley and hiding himself in a shed for three hours, hoping the police didn't bring dogs out in the winter. When he finally left the shed, there were no more busses running and he ended up walking to an all-night coffee shop and sitting up drinking coffee until the first bus ran.

Rob took the bus back downtown, shoplifted a sport bag and some nylons, then waited until it was time to catch his bus to the North End. He was wired from too much coffee but in a way he liked the sensation of hyper-awareness the danger and the excitement gave him. Up until that point his life had been pretty boring. He had dropped out of school when he was younger because he couldn't take the teasing. His grades weren't all that bad, he just for some reason didn't seem to have any common sense and people picked on him for it. And now he needed money more than anything in the world and there really seemed to be no jobs out there. So here he was, about to change his bad luck, about to take his destiny in his own hands for the first time in his life. He would buy the thing he needed, pay off his co-conspirators and then he would board the bus for Fort MacMurray and get a good paying job in the Oil sands and that certain special someone just may be proud of him again.

    As he sat in the back of the bus, Rob familiarized himself with the workings of the pistol. Maybe it was a good thing that he had gone to Ben's place, now he would really have a chance to learn how the gun worked when the shit really was about to hit the fan. When he got off the bus, it was a short walk to the bank and he waited for it to be exactly ten and ducked into the ATM and pulled the nylon over his head.

    Rob casually walked into the bank, nylon and all and just as he pulled out his gun a teller saw him and screamed. He let the gun go off twice and then pointed to each person in the room.

    "Anybody gets brave and they're dead!" He yelled. "Now fill up this bag, each of you!" He pointed his gun at the three tellers and threw the sport bag to the first one. Some money seemed to go in from each of them and then he grabbed the bag and ran out. There was a cab there so he got in it and pulled off his mask and tucked his gun into his belt. "Let's go, let's go!" He yelled at the driver.

"Where would you like to go?" The driver asked, seemingly not knowing what he wanted.

"Okay, for fuck's sake!" Rob yelled and counted out $300.00 from the bag and gave it to him. Just then there was a loud knock at the window and Rob nearly crapped himself. The door opened and the guy said,

"Hey asshole, you're supposed to get in my cab!" Suddenly Rob realized he had gotten into the wrong cab and was so flustered he got out and got in the other cab without reclaiming his $300.00. He chalked it up to a minor mistake, thinking there were thousands in the bag and the right cab sped off with him on board. He directed the driver to a downtown pawn shop and seemed to be in there for a while, then came out with a used black leather jacket on and a baseball cap he had bought and a box with a video game console and some games in it. He handed the $300 to the driver and watched him pull away, then got into another cab and sped off.

Rob had the next cab drop him off a few blocks away from where he was going and he hopped fences and ran through alleys until he got there. He was terribly nervous but he walked up and rang the doorbell, game console in one hand and bag of cash in the other.

"What the fuck do you want?" Came the reply from the young woman he had married three years ago at age twenty when they found out she was with child.

"I came to give Jacob this." Rob said and held out the console and games. "Don't get all pissed off at me, it's his birthday. I have something for you too."

"I don't know if I should let you in Rob, it isn't good for Jake to see you. All you ever do is let him down, you don't even have a job or anything."

"Hey, come on! I got my hands on some money, I got him a present. I'm going to give you most of the cash minus what I owe, then I'm going to the Fort to get some rig hand work. This time I'm serious."

"Like the man in the movie says, show me the money."

"Here." He said and opened the bag. There were piles of twenties and fifties and tens and fives in there.

"Okay, but you better be serious about getting a job and I don't want to find out you got this money from some rip-off." Rob went in and his little three year-old boy came rushing in yelling,

"Daddy! Daddy!" and gave Rob a huge hug. He gave him and even bigger one after his Dad gave him his present. In no time he had set it up and was happily playing away while Rob watched him from the kitchen of what used to be his home. Suddenly the phone rang and Amy got up to answer it.

"Mrs. Fletcher?"

"Yes."

"This is Sergeant Johnson of the Edmonton Police Service. Can you tell us if your husband is home?"

"Yes he is, but he's just visiting."

"Mrs. Fletcher, we have been staking out your home since last night. We have reason to believe your husband is armed and dangerous. We have a team of men outside, can we get each of you to come out with hands high and empty?" With that, Amy dropped the phone and let out a scream of fear. Instinctively, she grabbed her young son and took him to the bathroom and locked him in. Rob came to see what was wrong and she said in a panic,

"Rob, you bastard! What did you do?" Rob turned red and all of a sudden knew something was seriously wrong and that it had to do with the police. He went to the window and peeked out and saw the members of the tactical team outside with their automatic weapons. He set his gun down on the floor and walked to the front door. Both of them opened the door and stepped out. They only got about three steps and then two of the six officers in the front came up and held them at gunpoint, while the rest kept their guns on the house. The cops yelled at them:

"Is there anyone else in the house?"

"Yes but..." Before she could finish, the loud crack of a pistol was heard coming from behind them and all of a sudden the cops let loose with a volley of automatic fire, shooting every window and every crack and cranny of the front of the small house.

"Stop! Stop! Stop!" Amy screamed. The shooting stopped and she screamed, "My baby-my baby is in there. I locked him up-he must have gotten out!" No more sounds came from the house and the two cops that were watching Amy and Rob had to hold them and then another two came and handcuffed them, kicking and screaming at the cops, at each other and at God. On the way to the police station they were told the horrifying news, that Jacob had been killed. His mother was released soon after and went to her Mother's house where she spent the rest of her days in a fog of depression until one day her body seemed to simply give out and she died a young but horribly aged person. No counselling or medications ever seemed to have helped her.

As for Rob, his case came to court and he was charged with various robbery and weapons offences, but thanks to a deal he made to plead guilty in return for a lighter sentence, he got away with just 15 years in total. Prison life seemed to be good for him, he was able to finish his high school, he held a job that paid him a small amount to be held for his release date and he always seemed to be the one standing up for the little guy when the really nasty people were on their case. When he got out at age 34, he met a young woman and was soon remarried and he had two children. The boy he named Jacob and the girl he named Amy. When the youngest, Amy, reached her 21st birthday, Rob somehow felt that he had given back to the world all he had taken, and his final act was to end his own life, leaving enough insurance and other money behind to take his wife well into her Golden years.

| The Base Jumpers and Other Stories

MR. BAGGOT'S STORY

It was a slow night in the brand new Colonel Mewburn Veteran's hospital and supper hadn't been much to sneeze at. There was no hockey game on to watch that late fall evening and most of the men were asleep already even though it wasn't far past 8:00pm. The Doctors only really put the serious cases in this facility, but there were all kinds of these cases at the Mewburn. Mostly the hospital was full of Second World War and Korean War Vets but there were a few from the first World War, and one of the patients I had been assigned to was a long-bearded old man named John Baggot. He was a cheerful older gentleman, and he always seemed to enjoy my company. At the time I hadn't been as liberated intellectually as I am now and was studying First World War history through correspondence and was hoping to secure a position as a teacher of history in a high school when I was done.

I don't know why, but from a young age I had been fascinated with war. The idea of these gallant soldiers enduring incredibly horrible conditions from mud to lice to rats, and the enemy assaults. How anyone lived through all that and had gone on for as long as Mister Baggot had really inspired me.

Leif Gregersen

My job there as a pastoral care volunteer was to basically keep patients who didn't get many visitors company when they were able to respond to company. There were some who just didn't want to talk to anyone, and I had to respect that no matter how much I knew they needed a hand to reach out, I had to move on to those who were more willing.

Today when I went in to visit Mr. Baggot, or John as he had me call him, he had gotten up and was in his wheelchair and in a good mood. We started off playing a few hands of crib and then he dictated me a letter which I tapped out on his old manual typewriter for him. It was a bit of a sad letter. He had me put down that just a couple of days ago he had a heart attack and thought things were over for him. The letter did depress me, but then I also considered that anyone who could beat me in three games of crib couldn't be that close to death. He himself wasn't sad to say these things, and I knew it was the deep faith he kept close to his heart that got him through these times. What really was sad was to see the ones that had no faith, no family, no real hope who were nearing the end.

"So John," I said, as I finished up his letter and got him to sign it, "when exactly did you become paralysed?" The words of this question seemed to hit him harder than the words he said in his letter.

"Well, it was in France in 1917." I knew he wanted to end the answer at that point, but I really wanted to know how this strong and serene man had lost the use of his legs but not any of his courage. I pressed him:

"Do you not like to talk about it?" I asked.

"Well, I don't know if it really matters anymore. It has been so long. Let me think now. It was just about fifty years ago. Lord how time does fly. Here's the deal: wheel me down to the smoking room and lend me one or two and I'll tell you more." This made me chuckle. John rarely smoked, I knew telling this story was going to take him to a place he didn't want to go but as a friend of his who he knew had a fascination with the war, he was going to take the pain, and likely make a grand joke of it by the end of the story.

I took the brakes off the wheelchair, leaned down to John's height and asked him if he was ready, then gently pushed as he used his hands to help power the manual chair out of his room and down the hallway. As we went down the hall there were a few men sitting in other chairs or on benches staring out the windows, legs long gone or arms that were blown off or worse, amputated more recently because of diabetes or other ailments. Not many people understood why I came to a place like this to work for free but most of these poor older veterans were really the salt and light. They had seen so much, been through so much yet never complained or demanded anything. They were just about to a man the most gentlemanly, kind and caring people I had ever known. As I worked at this place off and on over a few years I started to feel quite against violence and war, but I really wanted to hear John's story.

We got down to the far end of the hall and wheeled into the smoking area and I again leaned down and told John I was parking him and pushed him up to a table with an ashtray, locked his wheels up and sat down across from him.

"Okay, Mr. Baggot. You owe me a story. Tell me about the War." I said, now trying to imitate him as I lit up my own cigarette and lit one for him.

"Let me tell you something, Sonny. You're a good kid. You've got the faith and I can see it in you. But I'll tell you right now, there is nothing about war that's easy. Nothing happy, nothing honourable about it. You go there in the muck and the filth and the dung and the rats and the lice and the maggots and you try and live. You keep trying to live and so you kill. A dozen times I took my rifle and blew some German kid's brains out. Blew them right out, for doing no harm to me. Can you understand that?"

"I can understand," I said sheepishly. "I can take it. Go ahead John."

"Well, I don't think you don't truly understand, but just listen and maybe you will. How I got into this wheelchair for what is now just about 50 years started out on a day not much different than this. I was in a bunker under the trench, sleeping. I had sniper duty that day, and would have to be completely on the ball, so I got all the rest I could. In some ways though, you never sleep. You kind of lay there wondering if you will live past the next day, and think about running or shooting yourself or even deserting. Not many guys did that I knew of, and all of them were caught, court marshalled and shot. I'm not ashamed to admit that I thought about it because any sane man would want any way out of the trenches he could find."

I sat listening in awe to his every word as he told me these things. It was odd but Mr. Baggot somehow seemed to change from his usual happy self to a dark and unhappy man.

"When I woke up on this particular day, I went to see my new Sergeant and he told me to go up the trench about 45 yard to where there were some bushes to hide in and take position. We synchronized our watches and he said in precisely 15 minutes they would make a diversion.

So, I made my way up, I took position and peeked up and I could see a damn machine gun set up and ready to go. Forty yards up from it was another and more and more of them. I knew something was up so I ran as fast as I could in boots full of water and mud back to tell the Captain the Germans were massing to attack. Normally they would shell us first but this looked like some kind of surprise they were planning for us. I got back to the Captain and he started yelling and screaming at me he even took out his pistol and likely would have shot me for disobeying orders but I told him about the machine guns and he looked as though he had wet himself. I think that this particular Sergeant had gotten his stripes about five days before after a quick-shot course in being an NCO."

"What about the men that were going to cover you? How many Germans were coming?" I asked, fascinated by his every word.

"Well, those men were okay but the rest of us weren't going to be unless we acted fast. We were short of men in our unit, some had been killed in a raid a few nights before, and five or six others had been sent back of the line in early stages of trench foot. Have you ever seen trench foot?" John paused to ask me. I shook my head indicating no. "Your feet start to rot right under you. The smell is what gets you first, smells like that French cheese they made. It's a horribly painful way to lose something."

"So the attack was coming and there was no way to fight it off?" I asked him, feeling not quite compassionate enough about the sacrifices these men had made.

"There were lots of men in the rear but they were nearly two miles from us. The Captain got on the phone and notified the artillery and our local airfield. All we had to do was hold out for a short while and we would massacre them."

"So did you end up getting a medal for warning the Captain?"

"You see, that's what's wrong with you kids. Nobody sees that there is no glory in killing, and no adventure and glorious victory in war. No, I didn't get any god damned medal!"

I was taken aback at how John said this, but I really wanted to bear the load he was letting off himself. There was a good chance that I was the first and very likely the last person to hear this story. "Now just listen to what I have to say."

"Sorry. Go on John." I said, blushing and feeling like a dumb kid.

"Okay, well, like I said, all we had to do was hold out. I told you that this was a surprise attack, but do you remember I mentioned there was a raid and some men were killed...?"

"Yes, I remember."

"Well, when the Germans raided they must have been measuring distances. They knew where we were and where our reinforcements were coming from in case of attack. WE were the ones who were sitting ducks, and you know why?"

"Mines?"

"That's the first right thing you said all day. Yes, the Germans had dug mines underneath our trenches packed to the rafters with high explosive. When the planned attack time came, in key positions they had set them off all at once, it was like the whole world had exploded right underneath our feet. The Captain was killed, two Lieutenants were killed, a Sergeant, four Corporals and untold numbers of Privates, except for me."

"Why was that?"

"I don't really know, no one really knows. What did happen was that I was thrown about forty feet along with about fifty thousand tons of mud and managed to land face up but unconscious. I stayed that way for a while, then when I finally woke up there were all these damn Germans everywhere. I couldn't think of what to do. They had passed me by because I looked dead and was buried. The only thing I could think to do was reach for a nearby rifle but I couldn't move anything. My arms, my face, my neck and all the parts of me that were buried were immovable."

"Was that when your accident happened? Were you shot?"

"That's the other funny thing. A lot of people get this idea that in a war people only die from enemy bullets. But in an attack, you can get hit by all kinds of things. You can fall in a crater and drown in mud. You can get strangled by barbed wire. Your own men can shoot you accidentally or on purpose. But no, this wasn't when I was paralysed. I guess I was just so full of fear and shock at the blast I just couldn't move. I lay there for what seemed like hours. A rat came and crawled over me, sniffing for any meat he could chew off my living bones. There was nothing I could do. I stayed there praying to God to let me die, let something happen, give me back my power to move. At one point a German came up and kicked me and looked in my eyes. I think he could tell I was alive but before he could put a bullet in me I heard the drone of an airplane and it must have been an artillery spotter because hell-fire started to rain down. The German ran for cover and not long after the reinforcements arrived and pushed the Germans back. By a million to one shot a soldier came by me and saw I was breathing and dug me out. They took me to a hospital and they found nothing wrong with me, except that they couldn't get me to move, even by jabbing me with a pin."

"What was going through your head?" I asked, in awe.

"There was constant shelling from far-off German guns. Sometimes there was even firefights just outside with stragglers from either side. The noise and carnage was the most confusing and frightening thing you could imagine men running, young men screaming for their mothers. At one point a German came running into the half destroyed building we were using as a hospital and a Doctor had to stab him with a bayonet."

"The Germans had massed a huge offensive and an officer had decided to come to the hospital and press-gang any man who could hold a rifle or a machine gun. He was raving mad, it seemed. He went to each man and a few of them, some with one injured limb or a missing eye volunteered. Then he got the me and went to turn me over to check my wounds. When he saw I wasn't injured he went ballistic. He ordered me put before a firing squad as an example to the others. Two men dragged me outside and tied me to a post. I can remember what it was like to look at them, my killers, after three years of war, here I was going to die from the hands of my brothers. Those men must have felt it too. Six men lined up, only one of them with a bullet, the rest with blanks, true to tradition. They fired and only one of them had an attack of conscience and aimed low. One was all I needed. He hit me here."

John opened his shirt and sure enough, there was a bullet wound in his stomach which surely must have severed his spine. I felt horrible that I had made him relive such a thing, but still he wanted to go on so I let him.

"I fell forward, they had thought I was killed. So much was going on that they didn't even bother to cut me down. The battle raged on all around me, all the excess men were taken and I half-stood there, bleeding to death. Many people must have died because of it but a French Doctor took me down and put me in an ambulance and took me to a hospital further behind the lines... he convinced my superiors I wasn't a coward... he... he..." As he said this his voice seemed trailed off and his head dropped. I could hardly believe what he was saying, this incredible story. I felt so honoured that he shared it with me, but I felt deep pain from guilt that perhaps I shouldn't have pushed him to re-live that horrible time in vivid colours.

"John! Are you okay?" I yelled for a nurse and took his cigarette out of his mouth. She came and took his vitals, he was breathing and his heart was beating. She had a Doctor come down later and the Doctor said this sort of thing can happen when the guys get wrapped up in War stories. I had no idea my questions could have done such damage and so I decided not to visit for a while. Every now and then I would call the Pastor I worked under for an update and each time I was told he didn't move, he just sat staring off into nothing, not even talking to the Pastor himself. I didn't get a chance to get down and visit again for some time.

A few weeks later, hoping somehow my presence could heal his wound, I went back to the Mewburn Hospital. There was my good friend John sitting in the hallway, staring blankly out the window at a garden. I felt horrible, I had always thought it would be so easy to counsel people, I had figured a couple of Psychology courses and watching a movie or two about analysis gave me the right to probe into people's minds. I couldn't have been more wrong. Time passed, and then one day I was in a pawn shop and saw a set of WWI medals. I bought all of them, likely paid too much but I took them home and found out what each of them meant from a library book. I took one for being wounded and one medal for valour out of the set and brought them down and placed them in poor old John's hand as he sat by the window. I heard a soft, quiet "Thank you" and that was the last I ever spoke to John Baggot. He died four days later, in his sleep. It took me another five years, but I got a degree in counselling, though I never met a man kinder and more brave than John Baggot.

THE END

lgregersen@ymail.com

Valhalla Books on Facebook

Made in the USA
Charleston, SC
06 July 2014